Naked to the Grave

By the same author

REMOTE CONTROL

DEATH TRAP

THE QUIET WOMAN

Naked to the Grave

HARRY CARMICHAEL

Saturday Review Press

NEW YORK

Copyright © 1972 by Harry Carmichael

First American Edition 1973

All rights reserved. No part of this work may be reproduced or transmitted in any form or by any means, electronic or mechanical, including photocopy, recording, or any information storage and retrieval system, without permission in writing from the publisher.

Library of Congress Catalog Number: 72-95554
ISBN 0-8415-0232-3
Saturday Review Press
380 Madison Avenue
New York, New York 10017

Printed in the United States of America

For Cecilia,
My wife

Give me the daggers. The sleeping and the dead
Are but as pictures.
Macbeth, II. 11.

CHAPTER I

IT WAS two or three minutes short of half-past five when Piper turned off Belsize Lane into Cornstalk Avenue—a tree-lined road curving in a gentle slope towards the higher ground of Rosslyn Hill. He was in good time for his appointment. Julian Davey had said he would expect him between five-thirty and a quarter to six.

The sun had gone behind a patch of cloud and there was the threat of rain in the air. As Piper slowed to a stop outside Denholme Court he thought he could hear a faint rumble of thunder far over to the west.

Half a dozen cars were parked in the residents' private enclosure fronting the main entrance to the twin block of flats. Ten yards farther along the avenue a telephone repair van stood with its rear doors open. A coil of wire lay at the edge of the pavement.

Piper switched off, removed his ignition key and checked the time. In his mirror he could see a blue Jaguar swing in a wide turn and drive into the private car park. He had seen the same car behind him in Belsize Lane.

A man got out—a sturdy man with blond hair and a pointed nose. He stood dangling his car keys and smiling as Piper came towards him.

Then he said, 'You're John Piper, aren't you? Recognized you from your photograph in the papers a couple of months ago.'

Piper said, 'You must be Mr Davey.'

'That's right. Glad I got here in time to meet you. Would've been home before now, but you know what it's like getting through the traffic at this time on a Saturday afternoon.'

'Yes, I do. Conditions certainly don't improve.'

As they crossed the flagged courtyard, Piper asked, 'Did you enjoy the match?'

Davey waited until they were inside the entrance hall before he said, 'Well, it wasn't bad. I've seen worse performances. The usual missed chances, of course, but taken all round the result was a fair one.'

The entrance hall had a runner of royal-blue carpet down the centre with parquet flooring on either side. At the far end of the hall there was a glass-panelled door through which Piper could see flower beds and an oval stretch of close-trimmed lawn.

Flats 1A, 1B, 1C and 1D faced each other in pairs on the ground floor. The lift was on the right, the emergency staircase directly opposite. Neon tubes boxed in the ceiling provided discreet illumination through Perspex covers.

Piper liked the atmosphere of Denholme Court. It was the kind of place with all the hallmarks of gracious living. He told himself that Julian Davey must have a prosperous business.

'... *Catering equipment covers a pretty wide field, I suppose. Wonder if it's an old-established concern or if he started it himself? Either way he must be making money...*'

They went into the lift and Davey pressed button 2. As the door slid shut, he said, 'Good of you, I don't mind admitting, to come here on a Saturday afternoon. I appreciate it very much.'

Piper said, 'Not at all. The Cresset people thought it advisable to get a valuation done before you and your wife went away next week. Never know what can happen these days.'

'That's what's been worrying me ever since I got the idea we might be under-insured. Since the last time I increased the amount of cover we've bought some new furniture and several pieces of silver that cost quite a bit.'

'Seems it's high time you increased the policy,' Piper said.

The lift stopped with the barest sensation of movement. When they got out, Davey said, 'I was surprised when Bill McLean arranged to send somebody with your special qualifications.'

It sounded like a compliment with just the barest hint of a question behind it. Piper asked, 'Why should you be surprised?'

'Well, you're hardly what I'd call—' Davey's mouth twitched in a smile but his eyes were still questioning—'an ordinary valuer. I thought about it after I spoke to you on the phone. From what I've read you handle more important things.'

'Sometimes . . . but they're the exception rather than the rule. Most of my work could be described as ordinary. This isn't the first valuation I've been asked to do for the Cresset.'

Davey nodded and smiled again. He said, 'I'm sure you're as expert at it as you are at most things connected with insurance. From the way McLean spoke he has a very high regard for you.'

'Nice of him to say so. He's a friend of yours, I gather?'

'Oh, we've known each other a long time,' Davey said.

He felt in his trouser pocket and brought out a leather key-case. Then he added, 'Don't know why I'm keeping you standing here when you probably want to get the job done and be off. You'll have a drink with me, I hope, before you start?'

'Not before,' Piper said. 'Perhaps when I've finished . . . if you don't mind.'

'Of course not.' He walked the half-dozen paces from the lift to the door of flat 2A and then looked back over his shoulder. 'Maybe you'd prefer a cup of tea or coffee while you're checking through my receipts and so on?'

'Only if you're making one for yourself.'

'Nothing surer. I promised my wife I'd waken her with a cup of tea when I got home.'

He put the key in the lock before he went on, 'She got to bed late last night and decided she'd have a lie down this afternoon to catch up on her sleep. Won't feel human until she's had her cuppa.'

Piper said, 'You attend to your wife and don't worry about me. I'm in no desperate hurry.'

'Three cups of tea are as easy to make as one. If you'd

rather have coffee that's no problem, either.'

'Tea will suit me fine,' Piper said.

He wondered why Davey was talking so much. The fact that his wife had spent the afternoon in bed was her own concern. Davey had no need to explain to a stranger. She might not like it if she heard he had been discussing her.

The thought was an idle one. It lasted only as long as Davey took to unlock the door.

When he had put the key-case back in his pocket, he said, 'Come on in, Mr Piper. Won't take me a couple of minutes to get things organized.'

Piper followed him across a rectangular hall, past a closed door on the right and into a well-furnished sitting-room. One panoramic window let in the amber light of sunset. The other looked out on a sky where dusk was spreading up from the horizon.

Davey switched on a pair of wall lamps. He said, 'Soon as September's here you can see the days drawing in, can't you? Take a seat and make yourself comfortable.'

He brought Piper a sheaf of documents in a folder and provided him with a small occasional table. All the time he carried on what seemed a compulsive commentary.

'... If you haven't got enough room, use another of these tables. Anything else you want, just say the word. OK?'

'Fine, thank you,' Piper said.

'Right then. I'll go and put the kettle on. Won't be five minutes.'

He left the door slightly open when he went out. Somewhere not far away, Piper heard the gushing of a tap ... the clatter of crockery ... random noises as Davey moved around, opening and closing a drawer, sliding back the door of a cupboard.

Soon there was the unmistakable sound of a kettle coming to the boil, then the other little noises of someone pouring water into a teapot, replacing the lid and standing the kettle down. Piper could hear it all very distinctly as he glanced through the contents of the folder.

... Receipts ... letters of valuation ... the original

insurance policy... an extension notice... several endorsements... a schedule showing that the sum insured had been increased in September of the previous year...

Julian Davey had spent close on two thousand pounds during the current year. On a slip of paper he listed other items which he considered were now inflated in value.

The total amounted to something between £10,000 and £12,000. Piper foresaw no difficulty in establishing that the higher figure would be acceptable to the Company. He had only to satisfy himself that the contents of the flat were as stated.

He heard the rattle of dishes, the sound of careful footsteps. Then Davey went past the partly-open door supporting a tray with both hands. Piper caught only a glimpse of him.

In the distance a radio was playing soft music, faint and far off. Mrs Davey must have woken up and this was her way of letting her husband know she was awake.

... Probably we disturbed her. She must realize he's brought someone home with him. Bet she won't be inclined to make polite talk with a stranger. All she wants is the cup of tea she was promised. He said she doesn't feel human until she's had her cuppa...

After Davey had gone another few steps he halted. Piper guessed he was outside the closed door in the hall. Judging by the rattle of crockery he was juggling with the tray while he tried to open the door.

Piper listened with half his mind while the other half noted dates and values of purchases made since the policy was increased last September. No one could say Julian Davey was tight with his money. Whatever he earned, he treated his wife generously. She had furs, jewellery and clothes in abundance.

The listening half of Piper's mind heard Davey go into the bedroom. The tray rattled again as it bumped against something.

Then Davey was saying, 'Here's your tea, dear. Sit up and take hold of the tray while I draw the curtains.'

Still faint and far away, the sound of the radio brought back memories to Piper of things long ago—things he should have forgotten long ago. They belonged to a time when the world was a different place and his life had been spent among different people.

. . . Funny how music can roll back the years. I can remember what happened as though it were yesterday . . . No, maybe not quite but it seems no more than a few months. Nothing else has the same effect as an old familiar tune . . .

He had no wish to meet Julian Davey's wife, to make conversation with a woman who had no wish to meet him. Better for both of them if she stayed in her bedroom until he had completed his inventory and left.

There he had a thought that came between him and his lingering recollections of the past. He felt glad that Jane was not the type of wife who stayed out late on her own.

Yet perhaps Mrs Davey had been visiting the home of a friend . . . perhaps invited for a game of bridge. No husbands had been there because it was a woman's game.

On the other hand it was silly to read too much into a chance remark. She might actually have been at home all evening. Davey had only said she got to bed late.

'*. . . Decided she'd have a lie down this afternoon to catch up on her sleep . . .*'

If they had no children she could do as she pleased so long as her husband had no objection. He could hardly object if she took a nap while he was at a football match.

A couple their age could well have children living at home. Julian Davey looked like a man between thirty-five and forty. Mrs Davey was probably a bit younger—perhaps a lot younger.

All the same the flat lacked that atmosphere of a place where there were children. Not difficult to tell. Always that intangible something when kids were around.

One thought succeeded another in those moments while Davey blundered into something in the bedroom and the tray rattled noisily again. Piper heard him say '. . . Sit up and put the light on, dear. I can't see where I'm going.'

The radio was still playing softly, the same tune at the same level of sound. It had become no louder when the bedroom door was opened.

Piper felt uncomfortable at the idea that he was eavesdropping. He had no right listening-in to a man and his wife talking together in their bedroom. The murmur of voices was so quiet it might have been coming from somewhere else.

If he wanted to avoid overhearing them he had only to shut the sitting-room door and concentrate on the papers he was supposed to be studying. Not that he had much chance of making out what they were saying.

. . . None of my business . . . I've nothing else to do but sit here and kill time until he comes back. Can't start the physical inventory in his absence. If he didn't want me to hear what they're saying he should've shut the door himself . . .

But the radio still niggled. It irritated all the more because it was so unimportant—like the elusive last word in a crossword puzzle. It should have become louder when Davey opened the bedroom door. Yet it was as distant as the murmur of quiet voices.

Against his will, Piper's thoughts ran on. Davey was blundering around in the bedroom because the curtains were drawn. On a bright day they might allow some light to seep in—enough to let him see his way in a familiar room. But it was dusk outside.

So the room must be pretty dark or he would not keep bumping into the furniture. He should get rid of the tray and switch on a light. There was bound to be a surface he could use—the dressing-table or the top of a set of drawers.

Some men were clever in business but stupid in other respects. And yet . . .

It could be that Davey was making all this fuss and noise so as to attract attention to himself, to advertise that he was a good and considerate husband. At worst, it was a harmless vanity.

Piper stood up and stretched. A second later he heard the click of a light switch in the bedroom.

Julian Davey was saying '... You must've been tired out, dear. What you need is an early night once in a—'

His voice broke off. Except for the distant radio there was no sound in the flat, no sound anywhere.

The music belonged to those days of long ago—music reborn decade after decade. A haunting phrase sang in Piper's head while he stood listening.

'... *You promised that you'd forget me not, but you forgot to remember ...*'

Then the melody was swamped by a noise of wild confusion: something landing heavily on the floor ... the smashing of dishes. And through it all ran Davey's voice crying out incoherently.

The tumult lasted only a moment. When it died away, Piper could hear once more the music of the radio. Now he heard it against the background of a man's stricken voice.

Over and over again, Davey wailed, '... My God, Pauline ... what's happened? Pauline ... Pauline, what's happened?"

He was making little whimpering sounds like an animal in pain when Piper reached the bedroom door. It was open just enough to let the light of a shaded lamp filter into the dimness of the hall.

For a second or two Piper hesitated. Then he pushed the door wide open and went inside.

The light came from a bedside lamp on a table between two single beds. Floor-length curtains had been drawn across a window filling almost the whole of one wall. In front of the window stood a dressing-table littered with cosmetics, silver-backed brushes and hand-mirrors, a box of coloured paper tissues which matched the shaded lamp.

One bed had been made with meticulous care. Julian Davey was standing beside the other.

At his feet lay a shattered cup and saucer, the fragments of a sugar bowl, its contents scattered over a wide area around him. Milk from a jug with a broken handle had splashed on his shoes. From an upended pewter pot tea mingled with tea leaves stained the carpet.

Those were the things that Piper saw in a fleeting glance as he went into the room. They registered indelibly on his mind so that afterwards he could picture them in every detail.

Afterwards memory painted in a wooden tray resting against the bedside table, a teaspoon that had landed on the floor several feet from where Davey stood. Afterwards Piper recalled the oddments on the table with the shaded lamp: a tiny bottle of pink nail polish and another of nail polish remover, some orange sticks, a couple of emery boards, several little balls of white cottonwool, a hand-mirror. The orange sticks and the cottonwool were new and unused.

All the bits and pieces were part of the composition of that mental photograph in which Julian Davey was the central figure. He had stopped whimpering. Like a man who had lost the power of movement he stood looking down at the disordered bed, his face pale and shocked.

There was a woman in the bed, a woman with blue-black hair spread out in tousled confusion on the pillow. Her eyes were closed, her features as still as though modelled in wax. A thin trickle of blood had oozed from the corner of her mouth.

She was covered up to the neck by bedclothes so that only her face could be seen. Once it had been a lovely face— sweeping jet-black eyelashes accentuating the pallor of her skin, delicate bone formation, a mouth shaped in sensual lines. Now she had only the cold pathos of death. Even from a distance, Piper knew beyond any doubt that she would never open her eyes again.

On the pillow near her head lay a pair of slim-bladed scissors tapering to a point as sharp as a dagger. The blades were red with fresh blood that had soaked into the pillow case.

With a feeling of nausea Piper remained quite still just

inside the doorway. He had no wish to go any farther.

For an endless time he was powerless to move or to think. He seemed unable to take his eyes off the dead face of the woman who had been Davey's beautiful wife.

In some other flat there was the murmur of voices again. In some other flat the radio was still playing that melody from long ago.

'... *Remember we found a cosy spot, and after I'd learned to care a lot, you promised that you'd forget me not ...*'

Nothing in the room had been disturbed. Piper could see no sign that an intruder had brought death to Mrs Pauline Davey. Only the bedclothes were in a state of disorder.

It was Davey who made the first move. Without looking at Piper, without giving any indication that he knew Piper was in the room, he reached out and drew back the bedclothes, inch by inch, until both of them saw how his wife had died.

She was naked to the waist—naked and despoiled like a mutilated statue. Her breasts were punctured with multiple wounds that had bled profusely. The top sheet was wet with blood. So were her shoulders and the base of her neck. To Piper it looked as though she were still bleeding.

In sudden terrible revulsion Davey threw the bedclothes over her again and stumbled backwards, his hands held out at full stretch. They were smeared with blood.

He said in a strangled voice, 'Oh, no ... no. Help me ... please help me ...'

Like a man demented he wiped his hands repeatedly on the eiderdown quilt in a frantic endeavour to get them clean. He was trembling violently when at last he turned and looked at Piper.

Outside in Cornstalk Avenue, car doors slammed not far away. Then an engine accelerated and the car passed Denholme Court and dwindled into the distance.

Davey stood listening until it could no longer be heard. His eyes were bewildered.

Twice he tried to speak. At a third attempt, he asked,

'Who could've done such a horrible thing? What reason did anyone have to kill my wife . . . to kill her like this? Why? Why?'

'I don't know,' Piper said. 'There's just nothing I can say.'

'But she was—' Davey looked down at his hands and shivered—'she was all right when I left here at half-past one. And the front door was locked. I'm positive I shut it . . . absolutely positive.'

'Had she gone to bed then?'

'Yes. She was almost asleep when I glanced in to say—to say goodbye.'

No expression of sympathy could ease his grief at a time like this. Piper said, 'The police will find out what happaned. You had better phone them. Don't touch anything in here.'

Davey's eyes shifted to his wife's still face framed in dishevelled dark hair. As he stared down at her his shoulders drooped and lines of despair etched the corners of his nose and mouth.

With something choking him, he said, 'It doesn't matter now. I don't care how it happened. Nothing matters to me any more. She's dead . . . that's all. Pauline's dead.'

A look of desolation settled on his face. As he groped his way to the door, he added brokenly, 'What am I going to do? God help me, what am I going to do?'

CHAPTER II

DETECTIVE-SUPERINTENDENT Rillett had a big solemn face and kindly eyes and thinning grizzled hair carefully brushed to cover his bald patch. He looked too gentle to be a policeman.

In a gentle voice, he said, 'I've heard quite a lot about you, Mr Piper. I don't want you to misunderstand me when I say I'm glad you were here. Somebody with an objective mind like yours could be a great help.'

'There isn't very much I can tell you that you don't already know,' Piper said.

The fingerprint men and the photographer had gone. Only the police surgeon remained. Piper could hear him at work in the adjoining bedroom where Mrs Pauline Davey had bled out her life.

Rillett walked to the sitting-room doorway and switched on the ceiling light. Then he went back to the window where the last red glow of sunset resisted the advancing darkness.

He said, 'What I got from Mr Davey was a somewhat incoherent account . . . as one would expect. The shock must've been considerable.'

It sounded almost like a question instead of a comment. Piper said, 'Any man who makes a cup of tea for his wife and then finds she's been stabbed to death is bound to be in a state of shock. I'd say he needs sedating.'

'Yes, indeed. That's why I've sent for his own doctor.'

'Where is Davey now?'

'In one of the other bedrooms. I advised him to put his feet up until the doctor gets here.'

With a hint of apology in his voice, the superintendent added, 'Gives us the opportunity to have a general chat about this affair . . . that's if you're not in any particular hurry.'

'No, my time is yours. The job I was supposed to do here for the Cresset Insurance Company would've taken me an hour or more, so I'm not expected home for a while yet.'

'Good.' Rillett's solemn face lightened in a smile. 'This job you talk about is as convenient a place to start as any. In your line of business, isn't a Saturday afternoon appointment rather unusual . . . especially one as late as five-thirty?'

'Well, yes, I suppose it is,' Piper said. 'But I didn't mind. Bill McLean asked me to do my best to fit in with Davey's arrangements.'

'McLean?'

'General manager of the Cresset. I gathered they meet socially quite often.'

'Was it McLean who fixed the appointment for this afternoon?'

'No. After he spoke to me on the phone I had a call from Mr Davey who explained that he wanted the inventory carried out before he and his wife went on holiday next week.'

'Leaving when?'

'Monday, I believe.'

'Couldn't the inventory have been taken yesterday?'

'He wasn't free then,' Piper said. 'And all this is rather puzzling. What are you driving at, Superintendent?'

Rillett used a little finger to probe inside his ear. Without any expression, he said, 'Nothing really, Mr Piper. You might say I'm trying to get aquainted with the people involved in this unfortunate business.'

'Including me?'

'To an extent—yes. After all, you were here when the murder of Mrs Davey was discovered. According to our medical friend in the next room it would seem that you and Mr Davey arrived not long after she was killed.'

Piper said, 'That confirms my impression. Although I've no real qualifications in the subject, I had an idea she'd been dead only a very short time.'

'Indeed? Useful to have a first-hand impression—'

Rillett scratched his other ear—'especially from a man of your experience. Several of my colleagues have mentioned your association with them in the past.'

'Always an amicable association,' Piper said.

'But of course.' There was no trace of pomposity in the superintendent's voice. 'I'm sure our relationship will maintain that tradition.'

He looked up at the ceiling light, his eyes remote. Then he asked, 'Why was the appointment made for half-past five? Why couldn't it have been earlier this afternoon?'

'Because he was going to the match at Highbury. Told me he never missed an Arsenal home game. And I don't see—'

'Neither do I, Mr Piper, neither do I. But I have a feeling the time factor may be all-important. Did Mr Davey tell you when he left here to go to Highbury?'

'Yes, half-past one.'

'Did he give you this information before or after he found his wife dead?'

'Afterwards. He was in a very distraught condition and he kept asking me why anybody should want to kill her.'

'Anything else?'

'Only that she was all right then and—' repeated out of context it now gave Piper an uncomfortable feeling—'and he was positive the front door had been shut and locked when he left.'

'Where was his wife at that time?'

Piper said, 'Forgive me, Superintendent, but I think it might be better if you asked him these questions.'

'It might be, Mr Piper, but I prefer—' Rillett's voice matched the look on his solemn face—'the answers I get from you.'

'They're only what I'm able to recollect. They can't be anything else.'

'Your recollections are good enough for me. At the moment, Mr Davey is scarcely rational. Until he's fit to be questioned I'm relying on you.'

With a nod and a fleeting smile, the superintendent added, 'Whatever you tell me, of course, will be in the strictest confidence. And please don't read too much into my somewhat roundabout approach.'

'I wouldn't exactly call it roundabout,' Piper said. 'As you wish. No two men see things the same way.' He clasped his hands behind his back, leaned slightly forward and asked, 'Now where did Mr Davey say his wife was when he left the flat at half-past one?'

It was no secret, Piper told himself. Julian Davey would confirm all this when he was personally questioned. Meanwhile Rillett had work to do and no time to waste.

Piper said, 'He told me she was in bed.'

'Sleeping?'

'Almost asleep was the expression he used.'

'I see. Now let's move on to five-thirty. You waited alone in this room while he made tea for his wife?'

'Yes. He was going to make a cup for me and one for himself when he'd taken her tray into the bedroom.'

Rillett nodded again. In a placid voice, he asked, 'Wouldn't you expect to be offered something a bit stronger than tea?'

'He did ask me if I'd like a drink,' Piper said.

'And?'

'I told him I'd rather not until I'd finished the valuation. So then he invited me to have a cup of tea or coffee.'

'Did you want either?'

'Not particularly . . . but I didn't want to appear rude.'

'So he, more or less, persuaded you?'

'In a way—yes. He explained that he was preparing a tray for his wife and I remember him saying three cups were as easy to make as one.'

'Talked you into it . . . m-m-m?'

'No, hardly that. But even if he did, would it signify anything?'

Superintendent Rillett said heavily, 'Perhaps not. Perhaps I'm merely stumbling around in the dark. Wouldn't be the first time.'

Like the replay of a sound-track Piper could hear once again Julian Davey blundering into the furniture while he talked to his wife who was already dead. And through it all ran an old familiar thread of music.

'... Sit up and put the light on, dear. I can't see where I'm going.'

The thought which grew out of that recollection was an obscene growth, a product of some insane nightmare. Its very presence brought defilement. As Piper cast it from him he knew it would remain on the borders of his mind waiting for the moment to return.

There was a sharp double-knock on the door and a man poked his head in. He had a ginger crewcut and a ruddy complexion dusted with freckles.

Rillet asked, 'Yes, Sergeant? What is it?'

'The doctor would like a word with you, sir.'

'All right. Come in and make yourself useful by drawing the curtains.'

With an air of old-world courtesy Rillett smiled at Piper and said, 'If you'll excuse me ...'

'Of course.'

'I won't be long. Sergeant Langdon will keep you company. Not much of a conversationalist, you may find, but none the worse for that.'

The superintendent gave Piper a nod and went out. He left the sitting-room door slightly open but he shut the bedroom door firmly behind him.

Sergeant Landon drew the floor-length curtains across both windows and then stationed himself beside one of the armchairs. He looked like a man dissociated from his surroundings.

In the adjoining room voices talked together in a murmuring dialogue of question and answer. Piper could make out nothing of what they said. Not that it mattered. If he were entitled to know, the superintendent would tell him.

... Hope I can get away soon. I'd rather not get involved in Davey's affairs. I'm sorry for him same as I'd be sorry for anyone in his position, but it's police business. The sooner I leave the better. Don't fancy the trend of the official mind ...

The bedroom door opened. A man's crisp voice said, 'That's about all, Superintendent. I can't do any more here so you can get them to take her away. Shouldn't be long before you have the PM report, but I doubt if it'll tell you much more than we already know.'

Rillett said, 'Confirmation is always useful. Meanwhile I've got an interesting line of inquiry.'

He came back into the sitting-room, nodded to Langdon and said, 'The doctor's finished now. When you've told them to remove the body you can go and see how Mr Davey's getting on. Stay with him until I call you.'

'Very good, sir. Would you like to know when his own doctor arrives?'

'Yes, I think I would. A word with the family GP won't do any harm.'

'Right, sir. Soon as he gets here.'

After Langdon had gone, Superintendent Rillett made sure the door was shut before he said, 'I've just been given some information that casts new light on this affair. Although I didn't expect it, somehow it hasn't come as a surprise.'

'I was never any good at conundrums,' Piper said.

'Oh, you won't have to guess. We'll get round to it eventually.'

Rillett poked inside his ear again. Then he asked, 'Where were we before I had to leave you?'

'Talking about three cups of tea. You seemed to think Davey might've had some reason for persuading me to have one.'

'Ah, yes. But I won't dwell on that. Instead I'd like you to think back to the time when you and Mr Davey entered the flat. Was the bedroom door shut?'

'Yes.'

'Completely shut? I mean could he have pushed it open or would he have had to use the door handle?'

'He did have to use the handle,' Piper said. 'From what I heard he had to balance the tray on one hand while he opened the door with the other.'

'You couldn't see him?'

'Only momentarily as he passed this door. I just got a glimpse of him holding the tray in both hands.'

'And after he entered the bedroom you heard him moving about?'

'Yes.'

'How long did that go on?'

'A minute or so. I wasn't timing him and so I can't say exactly.'

Rillett said, 'Naturally. You wouldn't anticipate . . .'

He stared up at the ceiling fixture as though he were counting the number of lights. Then he asked, 'Did you hear Mr Davey tell his wife to switch on the lamp beside her bed?'

'Yes.'

'And immediately afterwards you heard him drop the tray?'

'Not immediately. He also said she must've been tired out and what she needed was an early night. That was when the tray and everything on it crashed to the floor.'

'I see. Did you rush straight into the bedroom?'

'No, at first I wasn't quite sure what I should do. But a moment later I heard him calling out his wife's name as though he'd gone crazy and I knew something must be terribly wrong.'

'How long was it before you went into the bedroom and saw what had happened?'

'Only a matter of seconds,' Piper said. 'And now I insist on being told where all these questions are heading.'

Superintendent Rillett's solemn face took on a look of even deeper melancholy. He asked, 'Can't you guess? Doesn't a man of your experience know that we start off in a case of this kind by following a standard routine?'

'Yes. Before widening the scope of your inquiries you have to eliminate the husband.'

'Or the wife . . . if the position is reversed.'

'That I understand. What I don't get is the use of a routine that doesn't apply.'

'Why not?'

'Because Mrs Davey was already dead when her husband and I entered the flat.'

'So what? She couldn't have been dead very long.'

Piper said, 'The length of time is scarcely material. She died in this flat while her husband was elsewhere. We met outside here at five-thirty. When does the doctor say death took place?'

'Within the hour prior to his examination. And he arrived at ten minutes to six. Of course, the period he allows is an approximation. It could have happened quite a bit later than ten to five.'

'Might even make it well after five o'clock,' Piper said.

Something chilled the kindly look in Rillett's eyes. It lasted only a fraction of a second.

He said, 'The impression you got was that she was newly dead . . . wasn't it?'

Once again Piper could see her naked body outraged by a mass of wounds from which the blood had not yet congealed. The sheet covering her was still wet with blood.

So the police doctor's estimate of the time of death must be right. Pauline Davey could have died only minutes before her husband carried in the tea tray.

'I almost imagined she was still bleeding,' Piper said.

Superintendent Rillett nodded. In his old gentle voice, he asked, 'Were you able to see how she had died?'

'Not at first. The bedclothes covered her up to her chin. But I saw the blood-stained scissors lying on the pillow.'

'Mr Davey says he didn't touch his wife's body. Is that true?'

'He didn't touch her after I entered the bedroom. That I can say.'

'Did he go near her?'

'Yes. He pulled back the bedclothes. When he saw the state she was in he threw them over her again and I thought he was going to be sick.'

'Since the top sheet was soaked with blood he must've got some on his hands . . . m-m-m?'

'Yes. The sight of it seemed to revolt him. He wiped them again and again on the eiderdown as though he couldn't rid himself of the feel of it.'

'I'm not surprised,' Rillett said. 'Nasty business. When I was talking to him he kept looking down at a bloodstain on one of his jacket cuffs . . . or what I guessed was a bloodstain.'

'So you knew without asking me,' Piper said.

'More or less. But I didn't know how.'

'Well, now you do know. Does it help to clear the air?'

'I'd like to think so, Mr Piper, I'd very much like to think so . . . even if it doesn't make my task any easier.'

He stared into the middle-distance, his eyes sombre and depressed. Then he said, 'You're not the kind of man who betrays a confidence. That's why I'm being so frank with you.'

'I'd rather you weren't,' Piper said. 'This isn't my problem and I don't want to become involved.'

'But, unfortunately, you are involved. You're my only witness of what took place when Mr Davey returned home shortly after half-past five.'

'I appreciate that . . . and I've done my best to help you.'

'Of course you have. All I'm asking you now is to be patient with me just a little longer while the details are fresh in your mind.'

'You've had all the details.'

'Not quite. There's one question that you alone can answer. At least, I hope you can.'

'All right. What is it?'

Rillett moved his feet apart and rocked to and fro. He seemed in no hurry.

At last he said in a careful voice, 'Just this: did you notice if Mr Davey had a stain on one of his jacket cuffs before he went into his wife's bedroom?'

The nightmare thought that Piper's mind had rejected returned as he had known it must return. He said, 'A routine check on the dead woman's husband is one thing,

Superintendent, but this is going too far. You're suggesting that Davey might've come home before half-past five, killed his wife and left again in time to meet me outside . . . aren't you?'

'Bluntly, yes. As a possibility it has to be considered.'

'Why? What motive could he have had?'

'There's always a motive for murder. In a case of this kind the hardest task would be to establish opportunity. Remember the celebrated Wallace case in Liverpool?'

'Yes. But if Davey had been here only a short time before he drove up behind me someone would've been bound to see him come and go.'

'Not necessarily. Anyway, he might have been prepared to take that risk.'

Piper said, 'What you're saying is that he planned the whole thing in cold blood. If he did, do you imagine he'd have staked his alibi on the chance that he wouldn't be seen entering Denholme Court twice within such a short period of time?'

Superintendent Rillett held up his hand. He said mildly, 'Let's not get into an argument, Mr Piper. You may well be right. I'm more interested in your remark that he drove up behind you. Would you care to elaborate?'

'There's nothing to tell. I saw his car in my mirror as I came along Belsize Lane.'

'What make of car?'

'A blue Jaguar XJ6.'

'How did you know it was his?'

'I didn't at the time. But when I pulled up he swung into the private car park and waited for me. When I joined him he said he'd recognized me from a picture he'd seen in one of the newspapers.'

Rillett's sad eyes puckered in thought for a moment. Then he asked, 'Had you noticed this XJ6 before you reached Belsize Lane?'

'No.'

'But it followed you all the way from there to this block of flats?'

'I didn't say it followed me,' Piper said. 'It was behind me . . . that's all.'

'Aren't you splitting hairs? Changing an odd word doesn't alter the facts.'

'The facts—no. But the implication—yes. You make it sound as though he were waiting for me in Belsize Lane.'

'I have to consider possibilities,' Rillett said.

Piper felt a tinge of resentment. It was unfair to use him as a sounding-board.

He said, 'All this assumes that Mr Davey could have got from Highbury to Hampstead in time to do what you suspect he might've done.'

'Might've done—' the corners of Rillett's heavy mouth puckered in a wry smile—'is the operative phrase. However, time need not have been any problem. So far we have only his word that he ever attended the Arsenal match.'

'I'd already thought of that,' Piper said.

'Naturally. I'd have been disappointed if you hadn't.'

With a different kind of smile, the superintendent added, 'You should've been a policeman.'

'If I were I'd be asking myself why a man should want to get rid of his young and beautiful wife.'

'Can't you think of a reason?'

'Not off-hand. Can you?'

'Oh yes. But then I have the advantage of certain information that you don't yet know.'

'Are you going to tell me?'

'When you answer my question about Davey's jacket cuff. Did you notice whether it was stained or not before he went into the bedroom?'

There were footsteps and voices in the hall . . . a murmured instruction . . . a man saying '. . . Lift your end . . . now back a little . . . that's right. Easy does it . . .'

Piper had heard them come upstairs, their slow and deliberate movements in the adjoining room. He knew what they were doing and he had no wish to listen.

But the scuffing of feet impressed itself on his mind to

the exclusion of all other thoughts. Pauline Davey was on her way to a table in the mortuary where they would cut her open to establish the cause of death. The law had to be satisfied. The law took no heed that she had already been outraged enough.

Superintendent Rillett was listening, too. He waited until the mumbling voices and the shuffling feet were outside on the landing before he asked, 'Well, Mr Piper? Did you notice if there were stains on his jacket cuff?'

'No, I didn't,' Piper said. 'To be honest, I couldn't even be sure his jacket was stained after he'd handled the bedclothes . . . although obviously it must've been.'

'I wouldn't use the word obvious in this case.' Rillett shook his head. 'It's got all the signs of a real teaser.'

'Although you've discovered a reason why Davey might have wished to get rid of his wife?'

'Yes. But what a man might have done isn't proof. As you say, she was young and beautiful. Perhaps it wasn't only her husband who thought so.'

'Is that just a guess?'

'Call it an assumption based on one solid fact. The doctor sent for me because he'd discovered something which put a different complexion on the whole affair.'

Piper said, 'Don't spin it out. What did he discover?'

'It would appear—' the superintendent was choosing every word with care—'that Mrs Pauline Davey hadn't been alone in bed.'

He folded his arms and retired into himself again. His kindly eyes looked sad.

Then he added in a tone of regret, 'As they used to say in the days when chastity still had some meaning, she'd been entertaining a member of the opposite sex.'

CHAPTER III

By twenty minutes to eight, Mrs Davey's immediate neighbours had been interviewed. When Rillett returned to Scotland Yard he left Sergeant Langdon to question the other tenants of Denholme Court.

At eight-thirty the police surgeon's preliminary report arrived. It merely confirmed what the superintendent had already been told. After he had re-read it he drafted out the results of his inquiries so far.

... The ground floor tenants in 1B, 1C and 1D were out during the afternoon, returning home between half-past six and seven o'clock. At this stage they have no contribution to make.

On the top floor the occupants of flat 3A are a Mrs Coombe and her small daughter, Philippa. In the course of our conversation, Mrs Coombe mentioned that she is separated from her husband. Subsequently I learned from other tenants that she is regularly visited by a man whose Ford Cortina remains in the private car park all night.

She told me she went shopping locally about two o'clock and got back an hour later. From then until the arrival of the police she neither saw nor heard anything untoward. Philippa was at a young friend's birthday party all afternoon.

Mrs Wrexham occupies Flat 3B. She is a widow in her forties and carries on her late husband's business in Finchley Road. The shop normally closes at five on a Saturday but she felt unwell today and came home at four o'clock, leaving an assistant to lock up. Mrs Wrexham says she went to bed and slept until five o'clock. Nothing disturbed her during that time or in the next hour prior to the arrival of the police.

Mr and Mrs Morell are an elderly couple who live in flat 3C. Their hearing is not too good and a statement from them would be of little value.

Mrs Kimmerling in flat 3D is a semi-invalid whose husband looks after her. They are sure they would have heard the noise of a disturbance if Mrs Pauline Davey had cried out for help. My opinion is that too much reliance should not be placed on what they say.

The occupants of the flats adjoining No. 2A should have been able to provide useful information, but here again results were disappointing. None of them was able to further my inquiries.

A Mr Andrew Guthrie was alone in 2B all afternoon. His wife is visiting their married daughter in America and he lunched in town, getting home at a quarter to two. He spent the next hour writing his usual weekly letter to the family and then worked on some papers he had brought home from the office.

These tasks occupied his time until after six. He says he was too engrossed in what he was doing to pay any attention to outside noises. He cannot recall hearing the doorbell ring at flat 2A nor the sound of any door being closed.

Mr and Mrs Rolfe in 2D heard no one come and go, no voices on the landing. They went out for a walk some time before three, met some friends who live in the centre block at Denholme Court and were invited to afternoon tea. They did not return home until close on six.

Flats 2A and 2B are immediately adjoining. No. 2C is occupied by Neil and Deborah Heskett who state they have been on friendly terms with Julian Davey and his wife.

Neil Heskett says he thinks he heard someone shut the door of 2A about one-thirty. Mrs Heskett has a similar impression but could not swear to it.

She states that she went out shopping at ten to three. Her husband had intended going to his club but changed his mind and stopped at home to watch the sports programme on television. After an hour or so he dozed off and was awakened by his wife's return at a quarter past five.

Both of them say they heard Julian Davey talking to somebody on the landing not long afterwards. They heard Davey and the person who was with him go into flat 2A.

From the foregoing it will be seen that almost all the statements I have been able to obtain are of a negative nature. I only learned what the neighbours did not hear.

If Mr and Mrs Heskett's impression that they heard the door of flat 2A close about one-thirty can be relied upon, it merely confirms Julian Davey's assertion that he left home about that time. The person they heard him talking to outside his flat some time after five-fifteen is most likely to have been John Piper, who has already given me confirmation that he and Davey entered the flat about half-past five.

It is the period between one-thirty and five-thirty that has still to be accounted for. There is no evidence that Davey returned home prior to the estimated time of his wife's death.

I interviewed one other person who was in a position to see everybody entering or leaving the block of flats Nos 1A to 3D by the front entrance on Cornstalk Avenue. She is Mrs Elsie Wilson, an elderly widow, who lives in 1A on the ground floor.

Mrs Wilson spent the afternoon mostly at the window of her sitting-room which looks out on the courtyard fronting the entrance. She was sitting at the window from about half-past two until after half-past five. On only two occasions did she leave this vantage point: one was when she went to let in the caretaker, a man called Tom Sherwood, who had arranged to do some odd jobs for her; the second time was when she went into the kitchen to brew a pot of tea for him.

Sherwood confirms that he arrived at two-thirty. Mrs

Wilson gave him a list of jobs that kept him occupied until very nearly half-past five. At a guess he would say it was a quarter to five when Mrs Wilson brewed him some tea.

On each occasion she was absent from the window for little more than a couple of minutes. I find it difficult to believe that Mrs Davey's killer left during that second absence. It is stretching coincidence rather too far.

However, access to this block of flats can be obtained by way of a rear door which leads on to the gardens behind Denholme Court. Either a resident or a stranger could have entered and departed by this means without being seen unless somebody was looking out of a rear window overlooking the gardens. Detective-Sergeant Langdon is pursuing inquiries in this connection.

Mrs Wilson is eighty-three years of age but her faculties are little impaired. I have no reason to doubt the statement she made to me.

She remembers quite clearly that Mrs Heskett (flat 2C) went out at ten minutes to three. Not many minutes later Mr and Mrs Rolfe left (flat 2D). Mrs Coombe returned laden with shopping bags at three o'clock (flat 3A). Mrs Wrexham (3B) came in at four o'clock. The last tenant whom Mrs Wilson saw before Tom Sherwood finished his work and left was Mrs Heskett who came back at a quarter past five.

According to Mrs Wilson only one other person entered this section of Denholme Court and that was the boy who delivered the evening papers about the same time as Mrs Heskett returned. It will be noted that the details furnished by Mrs Wilson tally almost exactly with those provided by the tenants in question.

I was in flat 2A when Julian Davey was visited by his own doctor who prescribed some mild form of sedation to combat the shock of what had happened. Davey refused to be sedated on the grounds that he might not be clear-headed enough to remember exactly what had transpired before he left the flat at one-thirty and after he returned in the company of John Piper about half-past five.

The doctor considered Davey was in a fit state to discuss the death of his wife. I questioned him in the presence of the doctor, Sergeant Langdon taking notes.

Davey's answers agreed substantially with what I had been told by John Piper. The one thing on which I could get no corroboration was that Davey had actually attended the football match at Highbury. This, of course, does not mean he is lying. Very few of the forty-three thousand spectators who were at the match could prove they were there.

Photographs of the bedroom and the deceased woman are enclosed herewith. It will be noted that several items on the bedside table have been knocked over. I am of the opinion that this may have happened when her assailant snatched up the pair of scissors.

There is no question that this was the murder weapon. They are hairdressing scissors and, as can be seen from the photograph, taper to a fine, sharp point.

One blade is stamped with the name: *PAM 500*. Embossed on one handle are the words: RAZOR SILVER STEEL. In the other is the place of manufacture: *Nogent, France*. Overall length—10 ins. Allowing for a firm grip on the handles, the blades could inflict a wound to a minimum depth of $5\frac{1}{2}$ ins.

The bedclothes have been sent to the forensic lab for analysis. Their findings might help to show whether it was Julian Davey or some other man who shared his wife's bed.

No fingerprints were found on the handles of the scissors. It was obvious that they had been wiped clean. Marks on the top sheet of the bed indicate where they had been held while the prints were removed.

All the evidence points to the fact that Mrs Davey had little chance to struggle before she was stabbed to death. One wrist was grazed as though it had been gripped tightly and this could suggest that it was she who had grabbed hold of the scissors to defend herself. If so, they were either used against her while she was still holding them or they were wrenched from her. The outcome was the same.

Julian Davey states that his wife had no enemies that he was aware of. He is unable to explain why she should have been completely naked in bed. To the best of his knowledge she always wore night attire.

I did not acquaint him with the doctor's findings. At the moment I think it would be as well to wait for the forensic lab's report.

Medical evidence so far makes one thing quite clear: Pauline Davey had not been criminally assaulted before she was murdered. Whatever took place prior to the killing was with her consent.

Of this the doctor is quite convinced. If further proof were needed it would be the fact that her nightdress was found neatly folded under her pillow.

Routine inquiries are proceeding. At this stage I would only add part of my interrogation of Davey which I feel may be significant.

I asked him if he pushed the bedroom door nearly shut when he went in with the tea tray. He said he did not think so.

Thereupon I told him that is how it was when Piper came out of the sitting-room. Could he explain how he managed to go inside carrying a laden tray when the door was not open wide enough?

Davey: 'Well, I might've closed it a little once I was inside so that nobody could see into the bedroom.'

'What do you mean by nobody? Mr Piper was the only person in the flat . . . and he couldn't have seen anything if you had closed the sitting-room door.'

Davey: 'I didn't think of it—at the time.'

'Yet you thought of pushing the bedroom door almost shut although you were encumbered with the tray.'

Davey: 'Yes, I suppose I must've done. It's the sort

of instinctive thing you do in the circumstances.'

There seems no doubt that Pauline Davey had a lover. It would be helpful if I could establish that her husband had learned of the affaire.

On Sunday morning, Sergeant Langdon reported that he had interviewed every tenant in the main block of flats at Denholme Court. None of them could remember seeing anyone entering or leaving the end block by way of the gardens at the rear.

'... Of course, that doesn't mean a lot, sir. An ordinary person wouldn't attract attention.'

'And whoever killed Mrs Davey could've been in and out within a matter of minutes,' Rillett said. 'The whole thing probably took place around five o'clock. One of the tenants would've had to be looking out at that particular time ... which is asking too much.'

'So they can't help us to prove anything either way, sir.'

'Quite true, Sergeant, quite true. As I said in my report to the AC, all we've got right now is negative. The neighbours have only told us what they didn't see and didn't hear. A lot of to-ing and fro-ing took place but nobody had the faintest idea that murder was being done.'

Sergeant Langdon pulled at the stubby fingers of his left hand from thumb to little finger and back to his thumb again. Then he said, 'In one way, sir, Julian Davey's a lucky man.'

'How do you make that out?'

'Well, if Mr Piper hadn't been with him, there'd only be his word that he found his wife dead when he came home from the football match.'

'If he really did go to the match, Sergeant.'

'Yes, I've thought of that, sir. He might already have come back to the flat without anyone seeing him.'

Rillett walked to the window and looked out at the mellow autumn sky. With his eyes fixed on a patch of drifting cloud, he said, 'All right, Sergeant, let's pursue that thought. Are you suggesting he never intended going to the match, that the murder of his wife was premeditated?'

'No, sir. It needn't have been like that. He may have changed his mind and come home when he wasn't expected.'

'To catch sight of his wife's lover slipping out quietly?'

'It's quite possible, sir. When Davey went into the flat and discovered his wife nude in bed—'

'Please, Sergeant, don't use that word. It reminds me of those nasty little magazines published by young men who set themselves up as saviours of humanity. A woman with nothing on is naked.'

Langdon pulled at the fingers of his other hand. He said, 'Very good, sir. Whatever you say.'

'Dammit, man—' the superintendent turned sharply—'don't be so sycophantic.'

'All right, sir, I'll try not to.'

'See you do. Now go on from where I rudely interrupted you. Davey had just caught his wife—as the lawyers would say—*in flagrante delicto*.'

'If that's what happened, sir, we can imagine the rest,' Langdon said.

'Sure we can. But what we imagine took place isn't necessarily the truth.'

'All the same, it provides a good motive, sir.'

'I grant you that. Nevertheless, we mustn't make our ideas fit what little we know of the circumstances.'

'It isn't so little, sir. There's no doubt someone made love to Pauline Davey while her husband was out. Not long afterwards she was stabbed to death. If Davey didn't go to the football match—'

'You're rushing your fences,' Rillett said. 'You need one fact for a theory, two facts for a belief, and three facts to establish a principle. The principle here is proof. Isn't that what we're taught?'

'Yes, sir. I'm just trying to build on the two facts that we have got. Mrs Davey was murdered some time between, say, a quarter to five and five-thirty: between half-past one —when Mrs Davey's husband left the flat—and a quarter to five a man called on her and they made love. That much we do know.'

Superintendent Rillett shook his head. In a solemn voice, he said, 'That's twice you've described it as making love. Call me old-fashioned if you like, Sergeant, but to me love doesn't enter into that kind of relationship.'

'Maybe not, sir. But a euphemism is better than an obscenity.'

With a look of mild surprise on his big heavy face, Rillett said, 'I like that, Sergeant. You have unsuspected depths . . . even if your views would not find favour with modern trends.'

He smoothed a hand over his thin greying hair as though to make sure it covered his bald patch. Then he asked reflectively, 'How do we know it was some other man who visited Mrs Davey? Why couldn't it have been her husband who went to bed with her?'

'That would cancel out the motive for her death,' Langdon said.

'Only one motive. There may well be others that have nothing to do with the reactions of a jealous husband. If she did have a lover, why couldn't he be the villain we're looking for?'

'I suppose he could, sir. But I can't think of any reason why he'd want to do it.'

'Neither can I . . . at the moment. What's more I have a feeling that we may be allowing ourselves to become too pre-occupied with the sex angle. It's about time we started looking for a completely different motive.'

'What would that be, sir?'

Superintendent Rillett said, 'I haven't the foggiest idea. But a call on Mr Julian Davey seems to be indicated at this juncture . . .'

He looked like a man who had not slept very well. There were dark shadows under his eyes and he cleared his throat frequently after he invited Rillett and Sergeant Langdon into the flat.

As they passed the open bedroom door, Rillett noted that the bed in which Pauline Davey had died was covered with a dust sheet which hung almost to the floor all round. The other bed was unmade.

A bedraggled newspaper lay on the floor beside an armchair in the sitting-room. On one of the arms rested an ash tray half full of cigarette stubs. There was some ash on the carpet.

Davey said, 'I'm afraid things are a bit untidy but you can understand . . .' He moved his hands aimlessly.

The superintendent said he understood. '. . . Must be a very trying time. I don't think you should be staying here alone after what's happened.'

'No . . . no, I'm all right.' He made another restless movement and got rid of something that came into his throat. 'I'd rather be alone . . . for a little while, at least.'

'Of course. I won't trouble you any longer than is necessary. I just want to clear up one or two things that have occurred to me since yesterday.'

Davey rubbed his eyes. He said, 'More questions, I suppose. I'd hoped that was all done with.'

Superintendent Rillett said gently, 'You'll have to get used to answering questions, Mr Davey, I'm afraid. That's what an inquest is for.'

'Do I—' he coughed and swallowed and coughed again —'do I have to attend?'

'Unfortunately, yes. You'll be called on to give evidence of identification. What is also important is that it was you who found your wife's body. The coroner will want you to describe the circumstances.'

Without any expression, Davey said, 'I see . . .'

His eyes drifted to Sergeant Langdon as though seeking comfort. Then he asked, 'What is it you want to know, Superintendent?'

'Nothing that should cause you any difficulty,' Rillett said. 'We've questioned your neighbours who were at home around yesterday lunchtime and none of them seem to have heard you leaving at half-past one. Mr and Mrs

Heskett think they did but they're not at all sure.'

A changed look came into Davey's face. When he had scratched the tip of his pointed nose, he said, 'Correct me if I'm wrong, Superintendent, but are you suggesting that I lied to you, that I didn't go out at half-past one?'

'No, sir. Please don't misunderstand me. I interviewed the neighbours to find out what, if anything, they had heard during the course of the whole afternoon. Your coming and going was quite incidental. The fact that they didn't hear you leave could indicate that they wouldn't hear somebody else leaving. You see that, don't you?'

Julian Davey said grudgingly, 'Yes. And I'm not surprised they didn't hear me going out. I closed the door quietly because I didn't want to disturb my—my wife.'

'That's what I thought,' Rillett said.

He stood nodding for a moment or two. Then he asked in the same gentle, sympathetic voice, 'Did you go into the bedroom before you left?'

'Yes . . . I looked in to say goodbye.'

'Was your wife asleep?'

'Nearly . . . as far as I could tell.'

'So you didn't speak to her?'

'No.'

Rillett nodded again. He said, 'I know this is a great ordeal to you, sir, but there are certain questions I must ask however painful they may be. You do appreciate that, don't you?'

With a little twitch in his cheek, Davey said, 'Yes. I realize it's your duty.'

'And a very unpleasant one in a case of this kind. However, someone brutally murdered your wife and my task is to find that someone. I'll need all the help I can get.'

'Of course. Ask me anything you wish.'

'Very well, sir. I'm particularly interested in the weapon that was used. Do you recall seeing those scissors on the bedside table?'

The shadows under Julian Davey's eyes grew darker still. In a difficult voice, he said, 'I—I don't remember.

They may have been there. I've seen them on that table more than once.'

'Along with the manicure things and the hand-mirror?'

'Yes . . . but they weren't there all the time. I mean the nail polish and so on. Just occasionally when she had a late morning in bed and wanted to do her nails.'

'But she wouldn't have used hairdressing scissors for her nails . . . or any scissors at all for that matter, would she?'

Davey rubbed the side of his sharp nose. Then he said awkwardly, 'No, I—I suppose not. Probably she'd been using them for something else and just put them down on the bedside table for the time being.'

Superintendent Rillett bobbed his head and smiled. He said, 'That's as good an explanation as any. Don't you agree, Sergeant?'

From his place near the sitting-room door, Langdon murmured, 'Yes, sir, I do.'

He wondered why the superintendent wanted his opinion. There was bound to be a reason. Over the years he had learned that his superior had a reason for everything he did.

The smile on Rillett's heavy face changed to a look of regret. He said, 'I have one more question to ask you, Mr Davey—a very distasteful question but the answer could be most important. Did you go to bed with your wife before you left the flat yesterday afternoon?'

Something stuck in Davey's throat again. When he got rid of it, he said, 'This is too much. You're supposed to be investigating my wife's death. Her relationship with me can't possibly have any bearing on what happened while I was out.'

'Oh, but it can,' Rillett said. 'You have my assurance that it may be vital to these inquiries. When you've given me a straight yes or no, I'll tell you why I must have your answer.'

'You've—' Davey faltered and made a fresh start, the nerve twitching in his cheek. 'You've no right asking a thing like that. It's plain nasty to discuss our private life

... now she's dead.'

'There won't be any discussion. All I want is one word: yes or no.'

'But I don't see—'

'Please, Mr Davey. Won't you trust me?'

With a shaky hand Davey felt the back of his neck while he swallowed several times. At last, he said, 'I can't see that it makes any difference . . . but the answer is no. And that's all I'm going to say.'

Superintendent Rillett said, 'I don't want you to say any more.'

He gave Langdon a brief glance, turned back to Davey and added in a sombre tone, 'You're entitled to know the reason for my question although it's bound to distress you. According to the police surgeon, a man whose identity is at present unknown shared your wife's bed yesterday afternoon.'

A rush of colour suffused Julian Davey's face. Then he went very pale. He seemed to be having trouble with his breathing.

After he had been silent for a long time, he said huskily, 'That's the most damnable thing I've ever heard. To slander my wife after what some swine did to her is outrageous. If this doctor of yours dares to repeat—'

'It isn't slander,' Rillett said. 'It's the truth.'

'You'll never get me to believe it.'

'Perhaps not. But your feelings don't alter the situation. It happens to be true. I'm sorry.'

'How does he—' Davey had a struggle with himself and began again. 'How can he possibly know?'

Very gently, Rillett said, 'If I were you, Mr Davey, I wouldn't inquire into the details.'

'Why not? If this thing is true, my wife must've been killed because she wouldn't give in to the man who attacked her. I've the right to know if that's what happened . . . haven't I?'

'Yes, of course. But the medical evidence doesn't bear out

what you suggest. There is no indication that she was criminally assaulted. Whatever took place was almost certainly with her consent.'

Davey drew in a long harsh breath. He said, 'No . . . no, you can't prove that. You'll never prove it. I won't let anyone—'

The look on Rillett's face stopped him. He shook his head, took another long breath and began to tremble.

In little more than a whisper, he mumbled, 'Oh, my God . . . I can't stand any more. It was bad enough that she was dead but this is too terrible. What will people say when they get to know? I'll feel they're talking behind my back all the time. How could she? How could Pauline do this to me?'

Rillett said, 'Don't worry about people. There's a chance it may never become public knowledge. All depends on the circumstances which led up to your wife's death.'

'What circumstances? If she—' Davey gripped his hands together to stop the tremor—'if she had a lover he must've been the one who did it. When you catch him the whole thing's bound to come out. The whole rotten business will be in every newspaper.'

'At this stage only the murder of your wife will receive publicity,' Rillett said.

'But you can't keep the facts hidden. What happened yesterday afternoon can't be swept under the carpet as if—'

'We don't know what happened. We're not even sure of the motive. Right now it's all surmise.'

Davey put both hands to his mouth and stood breathing shallow little breaths while the moments passed. Then at last he roused himself.

His eyes were on Sergeant Langdon's freckled face, but he was talking to the superintendent when he asked, 'Have you anything else to tell me, any more questions, or is that all?'

'Not quite,' Rillett said. 'With your co-operation I'd like to take another look round the flat, a more thorough examination than I made yesterday.'

'Why? What do you expect to find?'

'I don't really know. Perhaps a motive for the murder of your wife, perhaps nothing. It's just a matter of luck.'

Julian Davey nodded. With empty eyes, he asked, 'Where do you want to start?'

'In your wife's bedroom,' Rillett said.

CHAPTER IV

THE search was painstaking and meticulous. Starting with the drawer of the bedside table, Superintendent Rillett examined every item, no matter how trivial.

There was a notepad that had not been used: a telephone directory: a phone dial pad which listed alphabetically names and numbers written in a neat script: an ash tray: a coloured plastic container labelled—*The Tablets . . . One to be taken at night.* It was empty.

Rillett held it up for Davey to see and asked, 'Do you happen to know what these were?'

'Probably—' Davey showed hardly any interest—'sleeping pills, I imagine.'

'Was she in the habit of taking something to make her sleep?'

'Very occasionally. I've known her take one when she had a late night and was over-tired.'

'Friday night, for example?'

'Perhaps. I was asleep when she came home, so I couldn't say.'

'Where had she been?'

'The Armada Casino. It's in Oak Hill Way.'

'Did she go there often?'

'Once or twice a week.'

'Alone?'

'Mostly. I seldom went with her. I've never been keen on gambling.'

'But your wife was?'

'Well, she got fun out of it . . . although she wasn't what you'd call a heavy gambler. The stakes weren't high and she wouldn't win or lose very much.'

'Did she frequently come home late from the casino?'

'No . . . just now and again.'

'How late would she be?'

'Maybe one o'clock . . . or half-past one.' Julian Davey was becoming restive. 'Would you mind telling me, Superintendent, why the hours she kept should be so important?'

'I just wondered if you ever felt worried at her coming home after one in the morning,' Rillett said.

'No, I didn't have any reason to be worried. She had her own car and she knew how to take care of herself—'

He chopped the last word in two and shut his mouth firmly. He looked as though he resented being made to appear foolish.

Superintendent Rillett said, 'Yes, of course . . .'

His face betrayed nothing. He put the plastic container back, shut the drawer and turned to the dressing-table.

The top displayed a brush, a comb, an aerospray of hair lacquer, several phials of perfume, a bottle of toilet water in a chequered box, cleansing wax in a small green pot of Grecian design. Some face powder had spilled on the plate-glass surface.

In the three drawers on the left-hand side there were several handbags in polythene wrappers, some costume jewellery, brushes and combs, note paper, a collection of sunglasses, two ball pens, a string of pearls in a white leather box.

Both upper drawers on the right-hand side contained an assortment of nail varnishes, hair combs, costume jewellery in profusion, ten or fifteen lipstick holders, little boxes of rouge. The bottom drawer held some lace-edged handkerchiefs, several packets of nylon stockings.

Sergeant Langdon had brought out a notebook and a pen. He stood tapping the pen between his square white teeth while he watched the superintendent begin to search the built-in furniture.

One half of the centre wardrobe was filled with day and evening dresses. The other half held fur coats, cloth coats, a mink jacket, two fur stoles.

Rillett checked every garment, patiently and carefully. He found nothing.

When he stepped back and looked up at the cupboard above the wardrobe, Julian Davey said, 'I don't know what you're looking for but this strikes me as being just a waste of time.'

'That's what most of my work proves to be. However, it's got to be done, all the same, because you never can tell. If you don't look you won't find.'

He lifted the hinged flap of the cupboard and stood on tip-toe. He could see almost to the rear wall.

The cupboard was full of shoes standing side by side in two neat rows. Rillett estimated there were fourteen or sixteen pairs—various styles in a variety of colours.

Davey asked, 'Are you going to examine each one individually?'

'No, I doubt if that will get us anywhere. So far nothing appears to have been disturbed . . . and we can't tell if any of your wife's possessions are missing.'

'You think robbery may have been behind this horrible affair?'

'Until I have evidence one way or the other I prefer to keep an open mind,' Rillett said.

He raised himself an inch higher so that he could get a better look. Then he reached into the cupboard and groped for something behind the farther row of shoes. When his hand came in sight, he asked, 'What's this we've got?'

It was a slim black handbag of the wallet type in patent leather—about ten inches by five. A gilt ring at each end had been meant to secure the strap handle but the handle itself was missing.

Before he unfastened the clasp, Rillett said, 'Right at the back where it wouldn't be easy to see. Couldn't have got there by accident so it must've been deliberately hidden.'

He moved away from the wardrobe, looked at Davey and asked, 'Any idea, sir, why she'd do that?'

Julian Davey said, 'If you look inside I think you'll find her reason.'

As the clasp snapped open, Sergeant Langdon came a

step nearer. He saw the thick wad of five-pound notes fastened with a rubber band along with some loose one-pound notes that had been stuffed into the handbag. He told himself that amount of money was a pretty good reason.

Rillett looked up at Davey and asked, 'You knew about this?'

With no apparent interest, Davey said, 'Not that there would be so much but I expected it would contain some money.'

'Why? Did your wife often keep cash in the top cupboard of her wardrobe?'

'Well, now and again, yes. I tried to tell her it wasn't a very safe place but she said there was never enough to cause her any worry.'

The superintendent said, 'I'd like you to watch me count what's here, sir.'

It totalled four hundred and twelve pounds—eighty five-pound notes plus twelve one-pound notes. At the bottom of the handbag Rillett also found a crumpled visiting card:

Mrs J. L. Davey
2A Denholme Court,
Cornstalk Avenue,
Hampstead, NW3.

The telephone number was in the bottom right-hand corner. Above it someone had written: *Tuesday 3 o'clock.* The handwriting was the same script as the names and numbers in the phone dial pad.

After he had replaced the card and the money, Rillett said, 'Something over four hundred pounds is a substantial amount to leave lying around in cash. Why should she keep it here instead of putting it in the bank?'

'Because it represented her winnings at the casino,' Davey said. He was still apathetic.

'What difference does that make?'

'The difference between your own money and borrowed

money. The casino isn't a charitable institution. Sooner or later they get it back.'

In a drab voice, Davey added, 'If you go on playing long enough the roulette wheel comes out on top.'

'Was that your wife's game—roulette?'

'Most of the time.'

Rillett clasped the handbag shut. He said, 'You had better take charge of this. Incidentally, do you know if she won the four hundred pounds on Friday night or is it an accumulation of several nights?'

'Friday night ... I believe. She told me she'd done pretty well.'

'When did she say that?'

'Lunch time yesterday just before I—' Davey's face grew dark and sullen—'before I went out.'

Sergeant Langdon wrote with slow deliberation in his notebook. When his pen stopped moving, Rillett asked, 'Who would know she'd won a large sum of money?'

Julian Davey said, 'Couldn't say. People at the casino might've known.'

'Players at the same table, perhaps?'

'Yes, they'd have a fair idea. Of course, anybody could've seen her being paid out when she cashed her chips.'

'Was she likely to have talked about the size of her win?'

'No, I don't think so. She'd been playing too long to get a kick out of that sort of money. All the regulars at the casino know that what you win one night you can easily lose the next.'

'That should be the text pinned above every gambler's bed,' Rillett said. 'It's fortunate for you that roulette isn't one of your weaknesses.'

Davey said gruffly, 'I'm not interested in any form of gambling. On the odd occasion when I did go to the casino it was only because my wife persuaded me ...'

He left the rest unspoken. With a wounded look in his eyes he turned away.

Rillett waited until Sergeant Langdon completed another

entry in his notebook. Then the superintendent said, 'Just one more question, Mr Davey, and then I'll be on my way. Have you ever suspected that your wife had a lover?'

Julian Davey stiffened. In one violent movement he swung round and said, 'That's twice you've implied that I haven't been honest with you. I resent it, Superintendent, I resent it very much. After what I've gone through since yesterday I'm in no mood for any cat-and-mouse business. If you have anything to say, come straight out with it.'

Very mildly, Rillett said, 'There was no implication intended, I assure you, sir. It was just a question that I thought I should ask. Of course, if you don't feel inclined to answer it . . .'

'I shouldn't need to—' Davey had to clear his throat again—'to answer it. By now you ought to know I've never had the slightest suspicion that my wife was being unfaithful to me. What's more I'm still not prepared to believe it's true.'

Superintendent Rillett said, 'That, sir, is your privilege. I won't trespass on your time any further. Good morning . . .'

Outside Denholme Court, he asked, 'Did it seem to you, Sergeant, that our friend wasn't surprised when we found over four hundred pounds in the shoe cupboard?'

Langdon said, 'It did, indeed, sir. Of course, he wouldn't be surprised if his wife often put money there.'

'Agreed. After all, she might've done. What niggles me, Sergeant, is that I could almost imagine he wanted me to find the money. Who says it was the late Mrs Davey who hid that four hundred and twelve pounds at the back of the cupboard?'

'You think he might've planted it there himself?'

'I'm tossing up my thought as a cock-shy for you to knock down,' Rillett said.

They got into the waiting police car. As Sergeant Langdon pulled the door shut, he said, 'If Davey's idea was to distract your attention, sir, it wasn't a very good idea. Who would know his wife was in the habit of keeping money in the cupboard?'

'A good question. If Julian Davey is our boy I'm getting more and more convinced it was a spur-of-the-moment job. When he found out she had a lover he blew a fuse. After the job was done he had to think fast and cook up something as an alternative motive.'

'Be helpful if we could trace her lover . . . providing we got him to talk.'

'Oh, yes. We'd know what time he left the flat and how long that was before the doc's estimate of the time she met her death.'

'Finding him is going to be the problem, sir.'

'If life wasn't full of problems we'd be out of work,' Rillett said.

Quinn of the *Morning Post* arrived at the office a minute or two after four o'clock that Sunday afternoon. In his typewriter he found a note from the news editor:

As you've only just fallen out of bed you won't yet know that Pauline Davey (32), attractive wife of one Julian Davey, a well-to-do manufacturer, got herself stabbed to death on Saturday afternoon. Motive unknown this far but she was naked in bed when it happened so a mind like yours can draw its own conclusions.

Julian lives at flat 2A Denholme Court, Cornstalk Avenue, Hampstead. So did Pauline until some time between four-thirty and five-thirty p.m. Saturday. Her present address is St Mary's Mortuary, Paddington.

If you get in touch with the PRO at Scotland Yard you may learn something to your advantage. I hope so . . . if you consider it an advantage to go on drawing your unearned income from this paper.

I'm taking a couple of days' leave but I shall open tomorrow's *Morning Post* with anticipation. For both our sakes, see that I'm not disappointed.

When he had read it twice, Quinn said to the typewriter, 'Hilarious . . . positively hilarious. He's as comical as a broken leg. If I was any good at clay modelling I'd make a little effigy of him and stick pins in it.'

The PRO was as informative as the official handout would permit. After he had given Quinn a digest over the phone, he added, 'I'm not supposed to go beyond my brief but there is one thing that should interest you personally. If I could be sure you'd keep it to yourself . . .'

'Monarchs have confided in me,' Quinn said. 'And I don't mean that variety act. You may safely unbosom yourself . . . as his lordship said to the housemaid in the pantry.'

'Well, actually it's nothing very secret but they didn't include it in the book of words. Seems an old pal of yours was in the flat when Davey found his wife's body.'

'Indeed? Since all the world's my friend, which old pal specifically are you referring to?'

'A man called Piper—John Piper. It's quite likely he'll have to give evidence at the inquest.'

Quinn said, 'Will he now? Much obliged, I'm sure. Some day I'll do you a favour . . . as the bishop said to the actress . . .'

CHAPTER V

THERE WAS no reply from Piper's home number. Quinn tried several times from a quarter past four until late that Sunday evening but the result was always the same.

When eventually he rang Detective-Superintendent Rillett he was told the superintendent had gone home. By ten o'clock, Quinn had to base his Column on Crime on the little he knew about the late Mrs Pauline Davey.

At nine-fifteen Monday morning, Piper's office phone was engaged. Quinn borrowed a cigarette from the man in Features, went back to his table and doodled on the margin of the *Morning Post* before he tried the number again. While he waited, Julian Davey was talking to Piper on the phone.

'... I'm damn' glad you were with me when I got home. Of course, it's just too ridiculous.'

'What is?'

'They think my wife was carrying on with another man and I might've known about it. The whole thing's an outrage.'

'Have they any proof?'

'Well, so they say. And the rest is even worse. Not that they put it into so many words but I can see which way their minds are working.'

Piper said, 'I can't. Do you mind telling me what this is all about?'

'Something that Superintendent Rillett hinted at. You remember him, don't you? He's in charge of the case.'

'What is he hinting at?'

'That I had a hand in—in what happened to my wife. Nothing definite, of course, nothing I could use—' The rest was lost as Davey cleared his throat noisily.

Once again Piper could see in his mind Julian Davey

passing the sitting-room door with a laden tray. Once again he could hear the rattle of dishes as Davey balanced the tray on one hand outside the bedroom. Once again there was that haunting thread of music.

'... *You promised that you'd forget me not, but you forgot to remember* ...'

The tray had a special meaning that took shape in his thoughts, time after time, and then vanished before he could grasp hold of it. If he could make it stand still for just a moment longer . . .

He said, 'What you're saying is that they think you murdered your wife.'

After Davey got rid of another obstruction in his throat, he said, 'It's damned absurd. She was the whole world to me. I still can't accept that—that she's gone. You don't know what it's like, old man. How could you know?'

Piper wanted to say he knew only too well. Recollections of the past had a habit of creeping up on him at quiet times if he let his thoughts wander. It was easier now to chase memory back where it belonged . . . but he knew all right.

Inside his head there was the squealing of tyres, a violent impact that scattered his wits into flying fragments, a lightning-flash picture of the open car door and the empty seat where Ann had been sitting beside him.

All so long ago . . . But nobody needed to tell him what it was like when someone died with brutal suddenness and two lives came to an end.

Yet talking about it would achieve nothing. He said, 'Let the police think whatever they choose. You didn't kill your wife so why should you worry?'

Davey said, 'It's easy for you to talk. I am worried.'

'You shouldn't be—if you didn't do it. An innocent man has nothing to be afraid of.'

'Don't be too sure. The police never give up. To solve a case there's not much they won't do.'

'Oh, that's just nonsense. Was your wife having an affaire?'

'Well, that's what the doctor is supposed to have told them. They say he found some kind of—' Davey faltered—'some kind of evidence. The idea makes me feel sick.'

The echo of Superintendent Rillett's voice repeated itself in Piper's thoughts—Rillett with a look of sadness clouding his kindly eyes: '. . . *As they used to say in the days when chastity still had some meaning, she'd been entertaining a member of the opposite sex.*'

Piper said, 'Assuming it's true, did you ever suspect that she was being unfaithful to you?'

In a plaintive voice, Davey said, 'Not for a moment. She never gave me the slightest reason to think there might be somebody else. I don't care what the doctor says, he must be wrong.'

'That isn't the point. If you had complete trust in your wife, you didn't have any motive. So take my advice and forget it.'

The phone made another husky noise. Then Davey said, 'I want more than your advice, Mr Piper. I'd like you to act for me.'

'How? What can I do?'

'You understand this kind of business. I feel as if I'm living in a nightmare. When I woke up this morning it took quite a while before I was able to convince myself that Pauline really was dead, that the whole thing wasn't just a bad dream.'

'I can appreciate all that,' Piper said. 'What I'm asking you to tell me is how I can help.'

'By—by asking questions. By finding out what led up to —to what happened.'

'The police are doing that. If the answer can be found they'll find it.'

'Perhaps they will . . . perhaps not. I'm not happy at the way they've picked on me. I feel too damn' vulnerable.'

'Don't blame them for that. They always investigate the husband in any case where his wife dies other than a natural death and there's every reason to believe a crime has been committed.'

'Yes, but—' The phone went silent.

Piper was becoming a little impatient. This affair had all the signs of getting out of hand.

He said, 'I don't see why you should feel at all vulnerable. You left your flat at half-past one Saturday afternoon and—'

'They're trying to prove I might not have done.'

'Let them. It makes no difference if you didn't leave until two-thirty or even three-thirty. Medical evidence has established that your wife was killed some time around five o'clock . . . possibly even later. What seems quite definite . . .'

The image of a man going past the sitting-room door with a laden tray flashed into Piper's mind like a vivid still photograph. He could see the tea-pot and the dishes, the flowered pattern of the tray. He could hear the distant sound of a radio.

It lasted only as long as the interval between one word and the next. Then it was gone.

'. . . is that her death could not have taken place any earlier than approximately a quarter to five. You were at Highbury and you didn't get back until half-past five.'

Almost against his will, Piper added, 'I know when you returned home. We met outside Denholme Court at five-thirty . . . as near as makes no difference.'

Julian Davey got something in his throat again. When he was rid of it, he said, 'The way you grasp these things convinces me more than ever that you're the man to help me.'

Piper said, 'If you need anybody at all in a case of this kind—and I don't say you do—why not get in touch with your lawyer?'

'Not on your life! That's just what the police are waiting for. It would be a tacit admission of my guilt.'

'But you haven't done anything wrong. You were at the match on Saturday afternoon—'

'How do I prove that? There's only my unsupported word I was anywhere near Highbury. They can say I knew my wife was involved with another man and ... oh, can't you see they won't look any further? It's not a question of the police having to prove me guilty. I'll have to prove I'm innocent.'

'That's not the way the law works,' Piper said. 'But you've had a bad time since Saturday and I can understand how you feel. So, if you want, I'll ask some questions in the hope that it'll ease your mind. I won't promise it'll do much good but at least I'll try. All right?'

'Yes ... thanks. I'm very grateful. Charge me any fee you consider justified.'

'We'll talk about that later. Before I do anything there's one question I must ask you.'

'Go on.'

'Did you—directly or indirectly—play any part in the murder of your wife?'

'No... no, I swear I didn't. You've got to believe that.'

Piper said, 'I haven't got to believe anything. If I find out that what you've told me isn't the whole truth, you know what I'll do with the information, don't you?'

Quinn's doodle took on the outline of a bed. Then he dialled the number again. He was trying to draw a naked woman in the bed when the phone answered.

'And about time, too,' Quinn said. 'Who's the lady?'

'What lady?'

'The one who was telling you the story of her life. I've been sitting here, man and boy, since twenty-past nine wearing out the seat of my trousers and wondering if it wouldn't be quicker to send you a telegram.'

Piper said, 'According to my watch it's only just twenty-five past nine. And you're wrong about the person who phoned me. It wasn't a woman. It was a man who's in trouble.'

'That makes a change,' Quinn said. 'Usually it's careless

women who get into trouble. However, even my brilliant observations won't buy shoes for baby so we must press on. How you been doing since the last time we met?'

'Fine, thanks. And you?'

'*Comme ci, comme ça.* As the poet says—My head is bloody, but unbowed.'

'You never change,' Piper said.

'So they tell me. I'm known as the Peter Pan of Fleet Street. How's Jane?'

'Very well. She was asking the other day if I'd seen you recently. When are you going to visit us?'

Under his breath, Quinn murmured, 'When your wife invites me . . . and not out of a sense of obligation for old times' sake.'

'What did you say?'

'Oh, just thinking aloud. I was running through my social engagements in the immediate future.'

'And?'

'Let's leave it for the moment . . . if you don't mind,' Quinn said. 'I'll see how I'm fixed and then we can make a date. OK?'

Piper knew what that meant. It was always the same but there was nothing he could do about it. Quinn was not Jane's type . . . however much she tried to preserve the bond between him and her husband.

There would always be that bond. But it became weaker as time went by. When a man got married, bachelor friends tended to drop out of his life. Quinn must know the old days were gone but he never spoke about it. Flippancy was the screen behind which he concealed his feelings.

'Yes, of course,' Piper said. 'Any time you have a free evening, let me know. Now what can I do for you . . . or was this just a social call?'

'Combination of business and pleasure. I tried to get you yesterday evening but had no luck.'

'Sorry about that. Jane and I went out for the day and got home pretty late. Anything important?'

'To me, yes. I've had a tip that you were on the spot when a Mr Julian Davey discovered that his wife had been murdered. Is it true?'

'Quite true. It'll teach me not to take on any work outside office hours . . .'

Quinn listened, coughed once or twice from habit and made little encouraging noises at five second intervals. When he had heard the whole story, he asked, 'Are you giving evidence at the inquest?'

'Yes. I received notification this morning. It's at eleven o'clock. Will you be there?'

'But of course. Lovely lady done to death in a block of luxury flats . . . blood all over the place . . . strong overtones of sex . . . An eye-witness account of the gory scene will give a real boost to Quinn's Column on Crime.'

'You mustn't quote me,' Piper said.

'When I can take all the credit for an inside story? You must think I'm crazy. And do me a favour, Mr Piper, sir. Cut out all the atmosphere from your evidence this morning. The way you described it to me is just tailor-made for my column. All I need is your private opinion as to what makes this whole thing tick.'

'Can't help you there. I've got no private opinion. Your best bet is to have a chat with Superintendent Rillett. I expect you've met him.'

'Solemn Sammy? Sure we've met. Did you know he was called Samuel? Father came from Wales. Grandfather was fire-and-brimstone Chapel . . . so they say. How much has the super confided in you?'

'Enough to tell me he has his reservations about Julian Davey. Scared the wits out of him, too. Davey was the man on the phone when you were trying to get me.'

Quinn said, 'The man who's in trouble . . . eh? What did he want?'

'Someone to lean on. My impression is he's got a guilty conscience. Of course, that doesn't mean he killed his wife. Among other things, he told me Rillett searched the flat yesterday—or part of the flat—and discovered more than four hundred pounds hidden in a wardrobe. Seems Pauline Davey regularly visited the local casino . . .'

This time Quinn listened in silence. Then he asked, 'What makes Davey think you can help him?'

'I don't know. But he's offered me a blank cheque. I've warned him I won't cover up anything I find out even if it's not in his interests, but that didn't seem to make any difference.'

'Where do you propose to start?'

'Denholme Court's as good a place as any. If Pauline Davey had a lover—and there isn't much doubt about it—finding him will take a lot of the pressure off her husband.'

'And plant it squarely on lover-boy,' Quinn said. 'If his cosy session with Pauline took place anywhere near five o'clock he's going to have a tough job convincing the police he wasn't the one wot done it.'

'Unless he left the flat much earlier and has an alibi for the estimated time of death.'

'Somehow I don't think he'll have an alibi,' Quinn said.

'Why?'

'Because it's obvious he knew she'd be alone all afternoon and there was no need to go dashing off. So my guess is he won't have had any other engagements. All he had to make sure of was that he was out of the flat and well away before hubby returned home and caught him with his pants down . . . if you'll pardon the expressive Americanism.'

With an artificial cough, Quinn added, 'I've just had an idea. How would you like me to go snooping around Denholme Court on your behalf?'

'For the usual *quid pro quo*, I suppose,' Piper said.

'The best pickings out of the story before any of the other vultures get near it—yes.'

'Nothing to be used until I give you the word?'

Quinn said, 'Cross my heart. Soon's the inquest is over I shall hie me hot-foot to Hampstead . . . ever tried hieing yourself with hot or cold feet? Maybe I'd better take a taxi.'

'You're a fool,' Piper said.

The inquest on Mrs Pauline Davey was well-attended by both press and public. Every seat in the small court-room was filled long before the proceedings began.

Julian Davey gave evidence of identification. He then described how he had returned home and discovered the body of his wife.

The coroner, Mr Peter Jobling, asked him: 'Did you return home alone?'

'No, sir. I was accompanied by a Mr Piper who had arranged to visit my flat at half-past five. We met outside Denholme Court about that time.'

'You entered the flat together?'

'Yes.'

'Was he with you when you found your wife dead in the bedroom?'

'No, of course not.'

'Why should you be indignant at my question?'

Davey said stiffly, 'Because I'm not likely to have invited a stranger into my wife's bedroom, knowing she'd be in bed.'

The coroner took off his spectacles, swung them between finger and thumb and looked at the jury. When he had put his glasses on again, he said, 'I need hardly say, Mr Davey, that you have my sympathy in this tragic affair and I can understand that you are not quite yourself . . . in the circumstances. However, we shall make better progress if you confine your answers to a simple yes or no wherever possible. Will you try to do that?'

'Yes . . . I'm sorry if I sounded rude.'

'Oh, that's all right. Where was Mr Piper when you went into your wife's bedroom?'

'In the sitting-room.'

'Did he remain there until you came out and told him what had happened?'

'No. When I discovered that somebody had killed my wife I must've cried out . . . although I don't remember it. The next thing I knew, Mr Piper had come into the bedroom.'

'Would you remember if you touched your wife's body at any time?'

'Yes . . . and I didn't. I just couldn't bear the idea . . .' Davey put a hand over his eyes and shivered.

The coroner waited impassively. Then he said, 'I appreciate how trying this must be but we have to establish all the facts to the best of our ability. Did you go near the bed at all?'

Davey took a little while before he said in a wooden voice, 'I drew back the bedclothes to see—to see how she had died.'

'You knew she was dead?'

'Anybody could see that. Besides, there was a pair of scissors all covered in blood lying on the pillow.'

After a moment's hesitation, Davey added, 'I didn't really want to look . . . but I had to.'

'Was Mr Piper in the bedroom at that time?'

'Yes.'

'What did you do when you decided that nothing could be done for your wife?'

'I'm—I'm not very clear about anything from then on. I think I covered her with the bedclothes again . . . but it's all rather vague.'

'Was it you or Mr Piper who phoned the police?'

'I did. Mr Piper said I had better ring them. And he advised me not to touch anything in the bedroom.'

The coroner took off his glasses and made some notes. With the pen held out like a pointer, he said, 'Let us go back to the time when you left the flat earlier that afternoon, Mr Davey. Was the outer door locked behind you?'

'Yes.'

'Did you lock it?'

'There was no need. It's fitted with a Yale latch. All you have to do is pull the door shut.'

'And you are quite positive it was properly shut?'

'Absolutely certain.'

'On your return at five-thirty were there any signs that the door had been tampered with?'
'No, none at all.'
'Any indications elsewhere of a forcible entry?'
In the same unmoved voice, Davey said, 'I saw nothing then or later to make me think the flat had been broken into. It was just the same as when I'd left.'
'So we may take it that the person who caused your wife's death either possessed a key or—' Mr Jobling leaned back and scratched his dewlap with the cap of the pen— 'or was admitted by her. Wouldn't you agree?'
After he had cleared his throat and swallowed with apparent difficulty, Davey said, 'It would seem so.'
'How many keys are there to the Yale latch on the outer door?'
'Two—as far as I've always believed. I have one and my wife had the other.'
'Have you looked to see if her key is missing?'
'Yes. It was in her handbag where she always kept it.'
'You've never known of the existence of a spare key?'
'No, we had only those two.'
The coroner said, 'Thank you, Mr Davey. I hope I shall not have to trouble you with any more questions.'

A Dr Maurice Thring, of the north-west police division, stated that, on Saturday, September 14, he had been called to flat 2A, Denholme Court, Cornstalk Avenue, Hampstead, and there found the body of a woman who was identified by her husband as Mrs Pauline Davey. In Dr Thring's opinion death had taken place within the past hour.
'. . . The deceased had been stabbed several times in the chest area. I formed the view that two or more of these wounds would have proved fatal.'
'How long would it take for death to ensue?'
'A matter of seconds. The multiple injuries were very severe, and there was massive internal haemorrhage.'
'Did you find anything in the bedroom or elsewhere that

could have been the weapon which inflicted these injuries?'

'Yes, sir. On the pillow there was a pair of bloodstained scissors. Because of some splitting of the various wounds it was likely that a weapon of this type had been employed.'

'Was this subsequently confirmed?'

'Yes, sir. On Sunday morning, September 15, Professor Young performed a post-mortem examination at which I assisted. He would be here now to give evidence before you, sir, but for illness. In view of the fact that I was present at the post mortem he trusts you will accept my account of our findings.'

Mr Jobling said, 'By all means, Doctor. I have Professor Young's letter apologizing for his absence and I see no reason why his inability to attend should, in itself, cause me to adjourn these proceedings.'

'Thank you, sir. Confirmation of my opinion that the bloodstained scissors were, in fact, the weapon used was obtained at the post mortem. The deepest wound which had penetrated the chest cavity of the deceased was almost five and a half inches in length. The overall length of the scissors was ten inches. Allowing for a hand-grip of four to four and a half inches, they could inflict a wound of this extent.'

'Did the blades match the other dimensions of the injuries you have described?'

'In every way, sir.'

The coroner gave the jury a sidelong glance over his spectacles. Then he said, 'Before we leave the subject of these wounds, Doctor, tell me this: could they have been self-inflicted?'

'Not in my opinion, sir. Two of them were of such gravity that had they indeed been self-inflicted the deceased would have been unable to place the weapon where I found it.'

'What you are saying is that, in those circumstances, the scissors would've had to be placed on the pillow by some other person?'

'Not really, sir. Any likelihood of suicide is not consistent with our findings at the post mortem.'

Mr Jobling removed his spectacles and made another

brief note. With the pen rotating between his fingers, he asked, 'Have you any other observations to make, Doctor?'

'Yes, sir. I should like to acquaint you with the results of a forensic laboratory test of the bedding. I asked for this test to be made because I was of the opinion that someone must've had intimate relations with Mrs Davey on the afternoon of her death.'

The little courtroom went very quiet. Piper saw the grim look that came into Julian Davey's face before he bent his head and stared down at the floor.

Through the silence, Mr Jobling asked, 'What was the outcome of the laboratory test?'

Dr Thring consulted a notebook. He said, 'It confirmed my opinion that a man had shared Mrs Davey's bed. Apart from the indications I had noticed, examination of the bed sheets revealed the presence of some hairs that were different from those of the deceased.'

'Different in texture?'

'And also in colour. She was a dark-haired woman. These were very much lighter.'

'Have you a copy of this forensic report, Doctor?'

'Yes, sir. But I understand that Detective-Superintendent Rillett also has one and will advise you of its contents in greater detail if you consider it necessary.'

'Then we won't pursue this aspect for the moment,' Jobling said. 'Anything else you think the jury ought to know?'

'Only that I found Mrs Davey's folded nightdress under the pillow.'

Very precisely, the coroner put on his spectacles. He asked, 'Do you mean properly folded or just rolled up and pushed out of sight?'

'Properly folded, sir, as though newly laundered.'

'I see. What was the deceased wearing?'

'Nothing at all, sir. She was completely naked.'

With no expression on his pale lined face, Mr Jobling entered the answer in his notes. Then he said, 'Just one more question, Doctor. Would there be blood on the person who caused the death of Mrs Pauline Davey?'

Dr Thring said, 'I think it is more than probable. Bearing in mind the condition of the scissors, I would say there must've been blood on her assailant's hand.'

In the same calm academic voice, the doctor added, 'And on his sleeve also . . . if he were wearing clothing at the time.'

'Supposing gloves had been worn?'

'The one which handled the scissors could hardly have avoided being heavily bloodstained.'

Mr Jobling asked the jury if they had any questions. A man with fuzzy hair and a slight stammer wanted to know if the deceased had struggled with her assailant.

'. . . Not just before she was killed. I mean, were there any signs that she tried to stop him taking advantage of her . . . if you know what I mean?'

The coroner said, 'I think I do. You are asking the doctor to say if he found indications that she had been criminally assaulted or if his opinion is that what took place between her and this man was with her consent. Is that your question?'

'Yes, sir.'

'Very well. What would you say, Doctor?'

'I found some bruising on the left wrist,' Dr Thring said. 'Also what would appear to have been finger marks on the upper right arm. That is all.'

'No other surface injury elsewhere on the body?'

'None whatsoever. I am of the considered opinion that intimacy could only have taken place by consent. Marks of violence that I would otherwise have expected to find were completely absent.'

Julian Davey raised his head, glanced around until he located the spot where Piper was sitting and then looked down at the floor again, one hand covering his mouth. He had the air of a man who knew everybody was watching him.

Detective-Superintendent Rillett's evidence consisted mainly of extracts from the forensic laboratory report. He was asked by the coroner if he had been able to trace the person who had had intimate relations with Mrs Pauline Davey.

'Not yet, sir. By way of elimination I questioned Mr Davey who informed me he had not gone to bed with his wife that day.'

'You searched the flat?'

'Yes, sir—on Saturday and again the following morning.'

'From your observations did anything appear to have been disturbed?'

'Apart from the bed in which Mrs Pauline Davey was found—no, sir.'

'You checked for fingerprints, I presume?'

'We did, sir. The only clear prints we obtained were those of the deceased, Mr Davey and the daily help—a Mrs Allen. Others which we could not identify were mostly smudges.'

'Any bloodstains elsewhere than in the bed?'

'No, sir.'

'You are satisfied that is where she was killed?'

'I have no reason at all to doubt it,' Rillett said.

Mr Jobling took off his spectacles, put them on again to study his notes and then asked, 'Were any strangers seen in or around Denholme Court that afternoon?'

'No, sir. All the tenants have been questioned but I learned nothing from them of any value.'

'Have you formed an opinion as to the motive for this extremely brutal crime?'

'Only a negative one. It would seem obvious that we can dismiss the idea of robbery. The flat contains many expensive items but nothing was stolen. Cash amounting to more than four hundred pounds had not been taken. I am, therefore, pursuing other lines of inquiry.'

The coroner rotated his pen between his thumb and two fingers and looked wise. He said, 'Let us hope, Superintendent, that you have early success.'

Mrs Marie Allen occupied the witness box for less than

two minutes. She was a sturdy woman of middle age with bleached yellow hair and masculine features.

She stated that she had been employed by the deceased as a domestic help since March. '. . . I did two days a week for Mrs Davey. She was always nice to me and I got a real shock when I heard what had happened. I'd been there that very morning. If anybody'd told me I'd never see her again—'

'Yes, Mrs Allen. We can readily understand your feelings. Was Saturday one of your regular days?'

'No, I usually worked Monday and Thursday . . . but last week my daughter had to take her baby to the hospital 'cos it stuck something up its nose and she couldn't get it out. That's the youngest one . . . I mean, my youngest daughter. Her sister's got no children and—'

'I'm afraid our time is limited,' Mr Jobling said. 'Can we just take it that you couldn't work for Mrs Davey on one of your normal days and so you made up for it by going to the flat on Saturday?'

Mrs Allen made a sound of exasperation. She said, 'Yes . . . that's what I'm trying to tell you. I couldn't go Thursday 'cos I had to look after the other children and that's how the beds wasn't changed and when I phoned Mrs Davey she said it'd be all right if I made it Saturday and not to worry and so . . .'

There Mrs Allen ran out of breath. The coroner asked, 'Which beds did you change in the flat?'

'The ones in the main bedroom.'

'Is that the room which was shared by Mr and Mrs Davey?'

'Yes. The other rooms don't get used all that much and so they don't have to be changed often. In the smallest bedroom the bed hasn't got no sheets at all and it's only made up if anybody's coming and that isn't once in a—'

'Yes, yes, Mrs Allen. Right now our sole concern is with the main bedroom. You are quite sure you changed the sheets on both beds?'

'Of course I'm sure! I didn't come here today to tell no lies. I was asked to say what I was doing in the flat last Saturday morning and it don't make no difference to me either way if—'

'You've been most helpful,' Mr Jobling said. 'I know you're a busy woman and so I won't detain you any longer. Thank you, Mrs Allen . . .'

John Piper described how he had met Julian Davey outside Denholme Court at approximately half-past five on Saturday, September 14, and what had transpired after they entered flat 2A. He also explained his reason for visiting Mr Davey's home.

'Were there signs of any disturbance in the hall or the sitting-room?'

'None that I noticed.'

'Was everything quiet in the flat?'

'Well, while I was waiting I thought I heard a radio playing . . . but I discovered later that the sound came from some other flat.'

'When Mr Davey went into his wife's bedroom you heard him cry out?'

'A minute or two after he'd gone in. During that time I could hear him stumbling against the furniture. Then he told his wife to sit up and put on the light because he couldn't see where he was going. Before that he'd asked her to take the tray from him so that he could draw back the curtains.'

The coroner said, 'I see. At that point you didn't have the impression he was talking to himself?'

'No.'

'And you heard all this quite distinctly?'

'I couldn't help hearing it,' Piper said. 'The sitting-room door and the bedroom door were partly open. I even heard what sounded like a light being switched on.'

'What happened after that?'

'Mr Davey started saying something to the effect that

his wife must've been tired out and what she needed was an early night. Then he dropped the tray and there was the noise of breaking dishes . . .'

'Go on, Mr Piper.'

'All the time, he was calling his wife's name in obviously great distress. I knew something must be very far wrong.'

'So you ran into the bedroom?'

'Not exactly. I paused outside the door before I went in. It was only when I heard him crying as though he was in pain that I felt entitled to see if I could be of help.'

Mr Jobling clasped his hands and leaned forward and rested both elbows on his raised desk. He said, 'I am asking these detailed questions, Mr Piper, because you entered the bedroom only moments after Mr Davey discovered the body of his wife. To all intents and purposes you were present at that discovery. Since you were not emotionally involved your evidence is likely to be more objective. Isn't that so?'

'Yes, sir.'

'Very well. Now I should like you to tell us what you saw when you went into the bedroom.'

Piper's account was clear and comprehensive. Mr Jobling had only one or two minor queries, the jury none at all.

No other witnesses were called. By half-past one the coroner had made his observations on the evidence presented. The jury then returned a verdict that death was caused by multiple stab wounds and that Mrs Pauline Davey had been murdered by some person or persons unknown.

Quinn and Piper met outside the court. They were walking together when Superintendent Rillett joined them.

He said, 'We three represent different facets of the same human condition, don't we?'

'I wouldn't know what that means,' Quinn said. 'To me "human condition" is just a phrase that sociologists beat the life out of on television. Did you get my message?'

'What message?'

'You'd gone home when I phoned yesterday so I asked someone to tell you I'd been on the line. Didn't he mention it?'

'Yes. He also mentioned that you wanted some information on the Davey case and I advised him to tell you when you rang again that you would get all the information from the press officer which was currently available.'

Rillett turned to Piper and added, 'You make a good witness, Mr Piper. I suppose you're glad to see the end of this business?'

'It isn't the end . . . so far as I'm concerned,' Piper said. 'Davey's commissioned me to make inquiries on his behalf.'

'Has he now?' The superintendent seemed hardly surprised. 'I wonder why he'd do a thing like that?'

'Perhaps because you scared him. He's convinced you think he was responsible for his wife's death.'

In a mild voice, Rillett said, 'Mr Davey can't possibly know what I'm thinking. Still, every man's entitled to his own opinion . . . and to have his own reason for being afraid. Didn't someone say conscience makes cowards of us all?'

'Shakespeare,' Quinn said. 'Through the mouth of Hamlet. It's in the bit that starts "to be or not to be" and goes on to talk about the dread of something after death which makes us go on living even when—'

'I learned all that at school,' Rillett said.

He looked at Piper and added, 'One has to be careful any time your friend's around. It's dangerous to ask a rhetorical question. Good day, Mr Piper . . . and good luck.'

When he had gone, Quinn said, 'You wouldn't believe old Solemn Sammy thought the world of me, would you?'

Without a pause, he asked, 'How would you like to buy me a quick pint before I set out for the wilds of Hampstead?'

Piper said, 'I'm afraid I can't. I have to get back to the office and clear up a couple of things. Then I'm going to pay a call on the Armada Casino. You might try to find out if any of Davey's neighbours frequent the place.'

'You think that's where she might've met lover-boy when her husband was at home?'

'It's possible. The employees of the casino may have noticed that she spent most of her time there with one particular man.'

'When do you expect to be at the Armada?'

'Between four and five. Won't be able to make it much earlier.'

Quinn said, 'If I pick up anything worthwhile at Denholme Court I'll ring you . . .'

CHAPTER VI

HE PAID off the taxi before he got to the flats and walked the rest of the way. Then he wandered here and there, loitering at the next corner, touring the gardens at the rear.

No one asked him what he was doing, no one questioned his right to be on the premises. He told himself anybody could have gained access to flat 2A.

... So long as the anybody had a key ... or was known to Pauline. If her lover didn't have one she must've let him in. Could've done the same for somebody else ... but not when she was in the raw. She wouldn't have opened the door without putting something on ...

There he had a new thought. Pauline Davey's lover might not have closed the door properly when he left.

... Maybe he didn't want to make any kind of noise in case one of the neighbours heard him. Maybe it was just accidental that the latch didn't engage and so the door only needed a slight push. If a prowler happened along and saw the chance of some nice pickings ...

But the question was why a prowler should have resorted to murder. Mrs Davey was probably sound asleep. A thief could have filled his pockets without disturbing her. There had been no need to go into the bedroom.

Yet an even bigger question was why the man who had made love to her should have stabbed her to death. Julian Davey had a motive ... if he knew she was being unfaithful to him ... or if he had come home too soon.

The weapon was ready to hand. But the choice of weapon made it almost certain that the killing had been unpremeditated. Only someone familiar with the bedroom could have known the scissors were on the bedside table.

... And it was dark as well. Piper says he heard Davey switch on a light ... presumably the table lamp. So whoever killed her had to know the scissors were there, had *to be able to find them in the dark. Unless the light was on and he switched it off after he disposed of Pauline* . . .

Either way it had to be husband or lover . . . if there ever had been a lover. If not, then Julian Davey was lying. He must have lied from start to finish. And that could mean only one thing.

Yet if she had not been unfaithful to her husband he had no motive . . . or, at least, no apparent motive. If the right questions were asked and they produced the right answers, appearances might prove to have been misleading.

. . . Another woman . . . financial difficulties that could be resolved by the death of an expendable wife who had money in her own right or who was heavily insured . . .

Perhaps no rational motive at all. Perhaps her death had been the outcome of a sudden quarrel that had ended when Davey snatched up the scissors in a wild, ungovernable rage and shut her taunting mouth.

It had happened before with other married couples. A wife went just too far, a husband lost control of himself and recovered his sanity when it was too late.

In the mellow sunshine of a windless autumn afternoon Quinn strolled through the gardens behind Denholme Court. They filled the angle formed by the two blocks of flats—lawns and flower beds set around a swimming pool, radiating tiled paths with bench seats at intervals. A central path ran between the two blocks and bisected the front gardens flanking Cornstalk Avenue.

Beyond the gardens at the rear there was a clump of trees. Farther back he could see two rows of numbered garages. Among the trees stood a garden shed.

It was padlocked. Through the window he saw a motor mower, cans of paint, fertilizer in paper sacks, a collection of tools, antiseptic and floor polish and some lengths of timber. Everything was neatly arranged so as to be accessible.

As he drew back from the window he caught an oblique reflection of his face in one of the dusty glass panes. For a moment he studied himself with the old feeling of distaste.

Straw-coloured hair that always looked untidy . . . pale, thin features . . . a general appearance of someone who needed to spend more time in the fresh air. There was a scar near his mouth where he had cut himself while shaving that morning. It stood out sharply against his sallow complexion.

He wondered if everybody else saw him as he saw himself. It was a depressing thought.

. . . You're like one of those illustrations of a Victorian consumptive. If you wore a wig and stuck a couple of grapefruit up your jumper you could play Mimi in La Boheme *. . . except that she's not supposed to have bloodshot eyes. About time you took yourself in hand, old boy, old boy, old boy . . .*

Someone came along the path from the direction of the swimming pool. He was a man above average height, slightly bald at the front and with an outdoor colour. There was clay on his shoes, smudges of drying earth on his bib overalls.

With a hint of suspicion in his eyes he looked at Quinn and asked, 'Anything I can do for you?'

Quinn said, 'Depends who you are.'

'My name's Mr Sherwood. I'm the caretaker of these flats. Who are you?'

Now everything about him was suspicious. The way he looked at Quinn he had no liking for what he saw.

'I'm Quinn—*Morning Post* crime reporter. You may have heard of me.'

'Can't say I have. Never read the *Morning Post*.'

'That would explain it,' Quinn said. 'As a complete *non sequitur*, may I say I've just been admiring the way you keep these gardens? Must take a lot of work.'

In a flat voice, Sherwood said, 'You're right—it does. But you didn't come here to pay me compliments. What is it you're after?'

'Some background material about the late Mrs Davey.'

'Weren't you at the inquest this morning?'

'Yes. But that dealt with facts. I'm interested in gossip.'

Sherwood made a little sound of ridicule. He said, 'I'm not going to talk myself out of a nice steady job . . . not for you or anybody else. If it got around that I'd been gossiping about the tenants, what d'you think would happen to me?'

Quinn said, 'It won't get around through me. I can't quote you, in any case, if it's only gossip or I might land my paper with a libel action. Like you I don't fancy joining the ranks of the unemployed.'

'Then just go away and leave me alone. There's nothing I know that would interest you or your paper.'

'Let me be the judge of that. All I want is a little something to add colour to my feature on crime.'

'Such as what?'

'The atmosphere of this place. Who's friendly with the neighbours and who isn't; who entertains a lot and who doesn't; who's married and who's living over the brush; who brought Mrs Pauline Davey home late at night and who visited her when hubby was out of the way; that sort of thing. Not that I'd mention any names—least of all yours.'

Sherwood looked down and stamped clay off his shoes. Then he said, 'You want a lot, don't you?'

It was two questions in one. Quinn said, 'Don't let it go any further . . . but I'm allowed an expense account. In a case like this I use it to pay for useful information . . . if you know what I mean.'

With his eyes roaming from Quinn's unkempt hair to his crumpled collar and stringy tie, Sherwood asked, 'How much?'

'How much can you tell me about Pauline Davey?'

'Only what I've picked up since I took over the job of caretaker.'

'When was that?'

'Eighteen months ago.'

'You can learn a lot in that time. Suppose I offer you a couple of quid for the bits I might be able to use?'

Sherwood's mouth drew back in a thin smile. He said,

'Suppose you offer me a fiver even if there aren't any bits you can use?'

'That's like buying a pig in a poke.'

'Sure. The pig might turn out to be a rabbit.'

To bargain would have defeated its own object. Quinn said, 'They say all life's a gamble . . . so you're on. And we'll start with gambling. I'm told Mrs Davey was a regular patron of the Armada Casino. How often did she go there?'

'I wouldn't know. I've never been in the place. But from what I've heard she wasn't the only one who liked a flutter.'

'Who else?'

'Well, there's Mrs Wrexham in 3B. She goes quite a lot. And I believe one or two others have a meal there . . . Mrs Coombe, for example. It's supposed to have a pretty good restaurant.'

Sherwood pulled down the corners of his mouth and added, 'She and her replacement husband have dinner at the casino once or twice a week.'

'What does replacement mean?'

'Her legal husband left her. It's no secret, at that. She told me herself he wasn't coming back.'

'Off with the old and on with the new,' Quinn said.

'Oh, she can ring the changes any time she likes . . . even if she has got a kid. Smart looking bird is Mrs Coombe. Not my fancy but there are plenty of fellows who'd run after her with their tongues hanging out.'

Quinn said, 'That's a quaint figure of speech. However, anybody else frequent the Armada?'

'Not that I know of by name. Most of the people who live here are getting on. A gambling casino is a bit out of their line.'

With his eyes probing Quinn's face, Sherwood asked, 'Why all this interest in the Armada?'

'Because Pauline Davey and her fancy man must've had a meeting place . . . and the casino is as good a spot as any. It wasn't every day they'd get the chance of hopping into bed together.'

The caretaker sucked in his lips as though he had a sour taste in his mouth. He said, 'Talking like that about a woman when she's dead doesn't seem right.'

'Depends how she behaved when she was alive,' Quinn said.

'Ah, that's all very well. I always found her pleasant enough. She used please and thank you . . . which is more than I can say for some people.'

A cynical thought came into Quinn's mind. This might be Pauline's only epitaph.

He said, 'Somebody else must've found her very pleasant in a different way. Whoever he was he'd hardly be one of your senior citizens. She'd want a man of her own age group—and lusty to boot.'

'Well, I never saw her—' there was no change in Sherwood's face but his voice was subtly different—'with anyone except her husband.'

'Not in the neighbourhood of Denholme Court,' Quinn said. 'She wouldn't want to be seen around here with her boy-friend.'

'That goes for the casino, too. They wouldn't make a point of meeting there regularly. She was too well-known. If they'd been seen together a lot her husband would've got to hear about it.'

'Unless fancy man was familiar to the others who went there—one of a regular crowd, as it were. People who spend a lot of time in a place get taken for granted. They can come and go, talk to anybody they please without attracting attention.'

Sherwood scuffed one foot through the layer of fallen leaves and looked thoughtful. He seemed unsure of himself.

Quinn asked, 'Does that ring a bell?'

'Not exactly. Like I say, I've never been in the Armada. Don't mind putting half a quid on a horse once in a while but I can't afford to gamble in a big way.'

'Then what were you thinking of just now?'

'Oh, probably nothing in it. I don't want—' he looked back along the path to the swimming pool—'I don't want to make trouble for somebody who's never done me any harm. It wouldn't be right.'

'Taking a fiver under false pretences wouldn't be right, either,' Quinn said.

'Does that mean you're trying to wriggle out of it?'

'No . . . it just means I want value for the firm's money.'

'You asked me to tell you what I knew about Mrs Davey and I've done that. What more do you expect?'

'Anything and everything that might have a bearing on the events of last Saturday afternoon,' Quinn said. 'You know someone with whom she was friendly. You're beginning to suspect they might've been more than just friends and—'

'That's not true! I don't suspect anything of the kind . . . so don't you go putting words in my mouth. Because I've seen her talking with one of the neighbours isn't to say there was any monkey-business between them. For two pins I'd tell you what you can do with your money.'

Quinn said, 'All right. No need to get excited. If this party was merely a friendly neighbour you won't be making any trouble for him. Who is he?'

When he had glanced back again along the path, Sherwood said doubtfully, 'I've got to be sure you won't drag me into it . . .'

'What're you worried about? You can always deny you ever spoke to me, can't you?'

'Don't think I won't! I'm not throwing away this job for the sake of a lousy fiver. If it gets back to the owners of Denholme Court—'

'Must we go all through that again? Whatever you tell me is strictly between us two. Now, for Pete's sake, who is he?'

Sherwood came a little closer. With scarcely any movement of his lips, he said, 'Man called Heskett. He and his wife are in 2C . . . opposite the Daveys' flat. They know each other pretty well—especially the two women. I mean, of course, they used to do. Mrs Heskett was very upset when she heard the news.'

'How about Mr Heskett?'

'Haven't seen him since last week. I'm not sure whether it was Thursday or Friday . . .'

'Where did you see him?'

'In the hallway—' Sherwood looked down and kicked some dead leaves aside—'outside flat 2A. He was talking to Mrs Davey.'

'Were they alone?'

'Yes, but there was nothing wrong in that. She was standing inside the doorway of her flat and he was outside. He waved to her and went into the lift as I came up the stairs.'

'Maybe he cut short the conversation when he saw you,' Quinn said.

'I wouldn't exactly say that . . . but you can think what you like.'

'What I think sometimes could get me locked up. When did you see them having this chat?'

'Thursday or Friday morning. I've told you I can't remember which it was.'

'Early morning?'

'No, it'd be after nine. Why?'

'I just wondered if Mr Davey was at home or if he'd gone off to business.'

'Oh, he left about a quarter to nine that day. He spoke to me here on his way—' Sherwood pointed beyond the clump of trees—'to the garage.'

'What does Heskett do for a living?'

'He's an architect . . . or something like that. I know he's connected with the building trade.'

'Does he always leave home after nine o'clock?'

With a touch of restlessness in his voice, Sherwood said, 'I wouldn't know. It's not my business to watch when the tenants come and go. What I saw that morning stuck in my mind only because of the way she was looking at him . . . and don't start making too much out of that.'

Quinn asked, 'How was she looking at him?'

'It's not easy to describe. The way a woman looks at a

man when they're not married . . . if you know what I mean.'

'Oh, but I do, I do,' Quinn said. 'If she listens to every word and laughs at all his silly little jokes, you can bet your shirt they're not husband and wife.'

The caretaker nodded. He said, 'Only an impression I got. Could be wrong, of course. I didn't think anything of it at the time.'

'What do you think now?'

'No more than I thought then. I don't want to make no trouble for anybody.'

'You said that before. Why should Heskett be in any trouble just because you happened to see him talking to a woman neighbour?'

Sherwood brushed one foot through the fallen leaves again. In an awkward voice, he said, 'Well, I know what some wives are like. If this sort of gossip got to Mrs Heskett's ears she might start thinking there really had been something between her husband and Mrs Davey. Could get him in hot water for no reason . . . and that wouldn't be fair.'

'You're too soft-hearted,' Quinn said. 'How old is this Heskett?'

'About the same age as Mr Davey—middle-thirty or thereabouts.'

'And Mrs Heskett?'

'Thirtyish. Why? What's her age got to do with it?'

'Maybe nothing. I just wondered. How is she for looks?'

'Quite attractive. Good figure . . . and so on.'

'As attractive as the late Pauline Davey?'

'No, I wouldn't say that.'

After a thoughtful pause, Sherwood added, 'Different type. But that doesn't mean Mrs Heskett isn't nice looking.'

'It just means that Pauline Davey was something special,' Quinn said. 'Have the police spoken to you since she was found dead?'

'Yes. Saturday evening.'

'What did you tell them?'

'A damn' sight less than I've told you,' Sherwood said. He wiped a hand on his overalls and held it out. 'It's about time I saw the colour of your money. So far you've been all talk.'

Quinn counted out five one-pound notes and passed them over. Then he asked, 'Who questioned you?'

'A copper called Langdon—Detective-Sergeant Langdon. He spent the whole of Saturday evening going round chatting to everybody.'

'Did you tell him you'd seen Heskett outside flat 2A the other morning after Davey had gone . . . and the look you saw on Mrs Davey's face?'

Sherwood folded the notes carefully and put them in an inside pocket before he said, 'No. Like I've been telling you it might not have meant a thing. And I don't go out of my way to make no trouble. Why should I get Mr Heskett mixed up in a scandal that he probably had nothing to do with?'

'Good for you,' Quinn said. 'If you happen to remember any more tit-bits, let me know. You'll earn yourself another pound or two . . .'

He went past No. 2A and listened outside the adjoining flat. There was a framed card on the door with the name: *GUTHRIE*. It had a gilt numeral and a letter mounted above it in the same style as the other doors.

The bell chimed once when he pressed the button and again when he released it. Inside flat 2B he heard someone moving around. After a long delay the door opened.

Quinn said, 'Good afternoon. Mr Guthrie?'

'Yes?'

'I'm from the *Morning Post* . . . and I wondered—'

'So did the last reporter who thought all I had to do was answer a lot of unnecessary questions. Well, I have neither the time nor the inclination.'

He was a short man with silver hair and bristly eyebrows and an overhanging moustache. His eyes were as fierce as the eyes of a pugnacious terrier.

'It'll only take a couple of minutes,' Quinn said.

'That's just where you're wrong. Ten seconds from now you'll still be wondering whatever it was you wondered when you rang my bell. Good day to you.',

With a curt nod he stepped back and shut the door. As he went away, Quinn heard him grumbling to himself.

No. 2D had a name-plate: *Mr and Mrs C. K. Rolfe.* Before he rang the bell Quinn could hear the murmur of voices.

They stopped when he touched the bell-push. Then a woman said '... make me a bundle of nerves. I can't go on being scared every time somebody rings the bell ...'

Her heels thumped briskly across a carpeted floor ... Quinn heard her tugging at a stubborn bolt. When it yielded at last she seemed to have trouble with the lock before the door eventually opened.

She was a handsome woman in her late sixties with well-kept hair, a trim figure and skilful make-up. Only a few tell-tale lines betrayed her age.

Quinn said, 'Sorry to trouble you, Mrs Rolfe ... but I'd be grateful if you could spare me five minutes. I've been asked to make some inquiries about that affair last Saturday afternoon and, so far, nobody else seems to be at home.'

'Are you from the police?'

'No, my name's Quinn. The *Morning Post* sent me.'

Without taking her steady, questioning eyes off him, she called out, 'Charles! It's a reporter. Will you talk to him?'

A man came along the hall—a corpulent man whose collar seemed too tight. He had a fat, pink face and he walked with the aid of a stick. By the time he reached the door he was breathing heavily.

In a husky voice, he asked, 'What is it you want?'

Quinn said, 'Anything you care to tell me about Mrs Pauline Davey would be very welcome. Most of the people here—'

'What paper are you from?'

'The *Morning Post*.'

Rolfe brought the stick in front of him, rested both hands on it and stood breathing in and out of his open mouth. Then he said, 'I'd have thought the *Post* was too reputable a paper to go in for muck-raking.'

'The main function of even the most reputable newspaper is to publish the news,' Quinn said. 'Murder isn't exclusive to the sensational press.'

'Don't give me a lecture. The facts of what happened are known to everybody. You're only interested in the sordid details. Well, I'm not prepared to discuss that kind of woman. To me she seems to have got no more than she deserved.'

Mrs Rolfe raised a protesting hand. She said, 'I'd rather you didn't talk like that in front of a reporter. We don't know enough to pass judgment.'

'I know all I need to know.' He looked at Quinn. 'Denholme Court used to be a respectable address. Now it stinks with notoriety and we won't live it down for a long time. Go back and tell your editor we'd like to forget the whole affair.'

'I'll do that,' Quinn said. 'But I'm afraid the story won't be quietly buried along with Mrs Davey. Somebody murdered one of your neighbours. That somebody has got to be found and put away. Given the right publicity—'

'Not by us,' Rolfe said. 'The less people say, the better for all concerned.'

He used his stick to prod the door. As it began to close, he added, 'I'd be glad if you didn't trouble us again. Good afternoon.'

All the people on the top floor were out. Quinn tried each of the four flats without getting any reply.

On his way down to the floor below he was thinking about Mrs Heskett. He had by-passed flat 2A because Julian Davey had already said all he was likely to say. In any case the odds were he would be at business. Apart from having work to attend to there was no sense in mooning around in the flat.

Heskett in 2C also had his business to look after. He would be out. If his wife was on her own it might be best to let her brood over recent events without being disturbed . . . assuming the caretaker's story had any foundation.

. . . *Maybe she didn't suspect there was anything funny going on between her husband and Pauline Davey. Then again, maybe she did. Could be she thought it would burn itself out. Might not have been the first time hubby had strayed from the straight and narrow* . . .

If the caretaker's imagination was not running away with itself . . . For a man to form that kind of liaison on his own doorstep was asking for trouble. Yet many a man when tempted enough threw discretion to the wind.

Quinn told himself it was possible that Mrs Heskett had never guessed. More often than not, the wife was blind to what was taking place right under her nose.

. . . *Question is what she'll do if she ever finds out. Perhaps nothing. So long as the police can't identify Pauline's lover, Mrs Heskett's best course will be to let the whole affair die a natural death. She's not likely to make a fuss and have her husband involved in the murder of his mistress* . . .

Unless . . . She might want to pay him back for his betrayal. If she did she would have to meet a share of the price in her own humiliation.

Outside flat 2C Quinn hesitated. There was a clumsily folded sheet of paper stuck in the letter box—an advertising leaflet printed in red. It had been there when he passed the door to call on Mr and Mrs Rolfe.

Three or four words were visible in bold capital letters: *FOR PROMPT SHOE REPAIRS* . . . The next word was lost in one of the twisted folds.

Without conscious thought he stooped to read the following phrase that ran diagonally across a thicker fold in the paper. At its thickest part it held the flap of the letter-

box slightly open.
OUR 24-HOUR SERVICE . . . WHY PAY MORE IF YOU CAN . . .

There he found himself thinking that no one ever really noticed the anonymous people who pushed circulars through letter-boxes, the youngsters delivering newspapers, the postman trotting up and down the stairs each morning. Nobody could describe them. They were the faceless people who came and went day after day without recognition.

. . . But you don't get any post on a Saturday afternoon. And that goes for circulars as well. Which leaves me with one of those youngsters on a newspaper round. I'm just not going to believe that poor Pauline was stabbed to death by some mad killer dressed up as a schoolboy . . .

The printed words merged into each other like his vagrant thoughts. He could hear a sound, faint and far away, inside flat 2C. It conveyed nothing to him but he listened to it while he read over and over again *WHY PAY MORE IF YOU CAN . . . WHY PAY MORE IF YOU CAN . . . WHY PAY MORE IF YOU CAN . . .* It was like a refrain in his head.

Then the far away sound became identified with a sour-sweet tang from the gap in the letter-box. He recognized the smell. He knew where he had heard that sound. Together they could mean only one thing.

Now the hissing seemed to be louder. And the stench in his nose was coal gas.

He felt his stomach turn over as he straightened himself and sucked in a breath of fresh air. Then he pressed the bell-push again and again and again in a wild jangle of noise.

There was no answer. When he stopped all he could hear was the hissing of wide-open taps, louder . . . and still louder.

With a hard fist he banged violently on the door until his knuckles hurt. All the time he knew it was no use. This was not the way. Soon it would be too late . . . if it was not already too late.

He was panting from the exertion when he began to beat on the door of flat 2C. He was still hammering without stop when it opened and he saw the angry fat face of the man called Rolfe.

Through a haze he heard Rolfe asking furiously, 'What the hell do you think you're doing? Have you gone mad?'

Then his own voice was saying 'Let me in. I've got to use your phone. I must ring the police. If we don't hurry she'll die.'

'Are you out of your mind? Who'll die?'

In that moment, Quinn's head cleared. He said, 'Your next-door neighbour. The place is full of gas. She's either dead . . . or she soon will be.'

CHAPTER VII

A PATROL CAR arrived within four or five minutes. By then someone had sent for the caretaker. He told the two members of the crew that no spare keys were available and their only course was to break down the door.

'. . . I've brought a couple of big screw drivers and a hammer. If you're not fussy about the amount of damage you cause it shouldn't take you long.'

They forced the lock without much trouble. When the door sprang open with a crack like a rifle shot and slammed back against the wall waves of choking gas poured out on to the landing.

Quinn held his breath and retreated to the top of the emergency staircase. Sherwood joined him a moment later.

The caretaker said, 'Nobody can go in there without some kind of mask. You wouldn't get ten yards.'

He was wrong. While they watched, one of the policemen came out of flat 2D carrying what looked like a wet towel. With the cloth held over his nose and mouth he paused, braced himself and then darted into the open doorway of 2C.

They heard his running footsteps . . . the smashing of glass . . . jumbled noises . . . a voice calling out 'Give us a hand, Bob! The gas is off and I've got the windows open.'

The second policeman went inside. When they came out they were carrying the lax body of a woman suspended between them.

Her face was deeply cyanosed and the veins of her neck congested. As they laid her on the floor, Quinn could see no sign that she was still breathing.

He remembered how Sherwood had described her. Now Mrs Heskett was no longer a good-looking young woman. Now she was nothing more than a bundle of limp flesh with a bloated discoloured face from which all life had gone.

One of the policemen began applying artificial respiration. The other went back into flat 2C.

Not long afterwards the ambulance arrived. An attendant administered oxygen while Mrs Heskett was being lifted on to the stretcher and carried downstairs. Quinn heard doors slam shut . . . an engine accelerate . . . the dismal wail of a siren fleeing along Cornstalk Avenue.

Mr and Mrs Rolfe went back into their flat. Mr Guthrie's door closed. The little group of people on the ground floor dispersed. Then only the splintered lock of flat 2C remained as witness of what had happened.

Sherwood said, 'Well, that's that.' He rubbed the bald front of his head as though it hurt. 'The way she looked made me feel sick. Wonder what made her do it?'

'There's always a reason,' one of the policemen said. 'Finding out why will be somebody else's worry. You better stick around for a while. The inspector might want to talk to you.'

'When d'you think he'll get here?'

'Not long. You can carry on with whatever you were doing providing you're available if you should be needed.'

After the caretaker had collected his tools and gone, Quinn asked, 'What about me? Do I have to stay here?'

The second policeman said, 'It was you who raised the alarm so you'll be wanted for sure.'

He poked his head into the doorway of flat 2C, took a few sniffs and added, 'Gas seems to have cleared now. You can come in and sit down if you like . . .'

In the next hour a lot of people asked Quinn a lot of questions. Eventually, there came a time when he said he was tired of hearing his own voice repeating the same story.

'. . . I'm beginning to think I should've minded my own business. You blokes spend a fortune advertising on the telly, urging the public to dial 999 if they see or hear anything suspicious . . . and that's all I did. Yet you treat me as if I was a candidate for the tumbrel . . .'

After a time they left him alone while men busied themselves in the kitchen. Then Detective-Superintendent Rillett arrived.

When he had spent ten or fifteen minutes with the officer in charge, he took Quinn into the dining annexe and invited him to have a seat. Rillett's manner was subdued and thoughtful.

Quinn said, 'Thanks all the same but, if you don't mind, I prefer to stand. I've got callouses from sitting. I've also got noises in the head from the endless interrogation.'

'Sorry about that,' Rillett said. He made it sound like a genuine apology.

'Me, too. Can I go now?'

'Not just yet. But I won't keep you long. Is there somewhere you have to go?'

'Yes. If my watch is right they're open. And, after what I've been through this afternoon, there's nothing I'd like better than to wrap myself round a pint of vintage bitter.'

With a half-smile that lightened his big solemn face, Rillett said, 'I'll be leaving very soon myself. If you wait a few minutes it'll be my pleasure to buy you a beer.'

Quinn pulled a chair away from the table and sat down. He said, 'Just shows how wrong you can be about people. I apologize for what I've been thinking. My time is all yours, Superintendent.'

'Then perhaps—' Rillett's smile dissolved into the deep lines in his face—'perhaps you wouldn't mind telling me why you were calling on Mrs Heskett.'

'She and the late Pauline Davey were friends as well as neighbours,' Quinn said. 'I was hoping I might learn something about the private life of Mrs Davey.'

'But you also visited some of the other tenants.'

'Only to find out if she'd been the subject of any gossip.'

'You knew we'd questioned everybody living at Denholme Court?'

'Oh, sure. I took that for granted. But people are

sometimes more inclined to talk to a reporter than a policeman.'

'And did they talk?'

'Not much. When I'd separated the chaff from the grain all I had was a teeny-weeny impression that Pauline might've had a thing about the man in flat 2C.'

Superintendent Rillett walked to the window and back. In a heavy voice, he asked, 'Are you saying Heskett and Mrs Davey were having an affaire?'

With a shocked look on his peaky face, Quinn said, 'Any resemblance between that idea and my impression is purely coincidental. If Heskett was her lover, then Heskett was the man who went to bed with her on Saturday afternoon. Maybe that wasn't all he did . . . but a lot of little ifs only add up to one big if and I'm not going to give Mister Heskett the chance to beat me over the head with a slander charge. Do I make myself clear?'

'Perfectly. But I'm afraid I didn't. Anything you say to me is strictly between ourselves. Heskett won't even know we've been discussing him.'

'I'll take your word for it,' Quinn said.

'And I'll take yours. It cuts both ways, remember. No talk unless I give you the OK. Understood?'

'Sure. I get the message. Has Heskett been told about his wife?'

'Yes. He went straight to the hospital. For all I know he may still be there.'

'Anyone spoken to him?'

'Sergeant Langdon asked a few questions. They're the counterpart of those I'd like to ask you. What time did you get here?'

'After two. I wandered around for a while before I—'

'How long after two?'

'Couldn't really say. Might've been a quarter past or twenty past. Does it matter?'

'It may prove to be very important,' Rillett said. 'According to Heskett he left home about two-fifteen after lunching with his wife. I thought you might've seen him leaving.'

Quinn told himself the conversation was leading into deep waters. He asked, 'Does he always come home for lunch?'

'No. Says he did so today because his wife phoned him at the office to say she was feeling a bit low. Seems she'd been depressed by the death of Mrs Davey.'

'Was his wife all right when he left her?'

'Apparently so. We've questioned the neighbours but nobody saw her at all today.'

'Which means Heskett's the only one who knows what took place in this flat,' Quinn said. 'If his wife doesn't recover . . .'

Sadness darkened the superintendent's eyes. In a tone of regret, he said, 'I'm afraid Mrs Heskett can't help us. She was dead when they got her to the hospital.'

The death of a stranger should have had little or no effect on Quinn. He had never met the woman. No emotional ties linked them together. Yet it was he who had called the police . . . and he had been present when they carried her out of the gas-filled flat. That formed some kind of bond. They shared those moments on the landing outside flat 2C—those moments when the paths of the living and the dead had crossed.

Maybe no one else grieved for Mrs Heskett. Maybe only a policeman and a reporter felt sad at the death of a woman who had lost the will to live, who gave up the struggle when she found there was nothing worth living for.

. . . Another suicide, another inquest . . . another entry in the coroner's record. If Heskett had quarrelled with his wife when he came home for lunch and if that quarrel had driven her to self-destruction, no one would ever know . . .

Superintendent Rillett said, 'The affair is a little more complicated than it seemed at first. In the kitchen we found an empty plastic container with a label which said it had held sleeping pills. There was also a glass with a few drops of whisky in the bottom.'

'That doesn't sound like a complication,' Quinn said.

'Wasn't she in the habit of taking sleeping pills?'

'Recently—yes. We got her doctor's name from the chemist and it transpires she'd been given a prescription for Quinalbarbitone capsules because she complained she wasn't sleeping very well. Quinalbarb is a short-acting hypnotic commonly prescribed for simple insomnia and anxiety states ... and the doctor says that's what she was suffering from—anxiety.'

'Did he discover what she was anxious about?'

'Not from her. But his opinion is that she was unhappy about her relationship with her husband.'

'Or her husband's relationship with another woman,' Quinn said.

'That's a reasonable assumption. We're also entitled to assume that she wouldn't have put her head in the gas oven if she could've used sleeping pills instead. But there weren't enough.'

'How do you know?'

'We asked the path lab at the hospital to do a test. When they examined the stomach contents they found a small amount of alcohol along with a quantity of Quinalbarb. Their estimate is that she'd probably swallowed something over 300 milligrams—that's roughly four of the capsules her doctor had prescribed.'

'Wouldn't that have done the trick?'

'In itself, most unlikely. Probably have put her into nothing more than a heavy sleep. Taken in conjunction with alcohol, however, the effects are sometimes unpredictable.'

'From her point of view, too unpredictable,' Quinn said. 'Wonder why she bothered to take them at all?'

The superintendent placed one hand on top of the other, fingers extended, and rubbed them together as though he felt cold. He said, 'The suggestion is that she put herself to sleep to avoid any chance she might change her mind.'

'If she had that thought, she couldn't have been finally determined, could she?'

'Perhaps not. Perhaps she half-hoped somebody would

walk in before it was too late. Many intended suicides don't realize how rapidly fatal a massive concentration of gas can be.'

'If that's what she was really hoping there would be only one somebody she wanted,' Quinn said.

He had a feeling of frustration. A woman was dead and they were discussing what she had felt and thought and hoped in the last moments of her life as though it made any difference. If it did . . .

He asked, 'How long would it be before this Quinalbarb stuff put her out?'

Rillett separated his hands and passed them over his grizzled hair. He said, 'Fifteen to twenty minutes.'

'What does it taste like?'

'Bitterish.'

'Would it be noticeable if it were dissolved in whisky?'

'Maybe not.' Rillett seemed distantly amused. 'Why?'

Quinn said, 'You know damn' well why. From the time we came into this room you've been talking all round the houses. Well, I don't like being kidded by anyone—even a detective-superintendent. What you suspect is that she could have been given the drug without her knowledge. Isn't that so?'

'Not entirely. But I admit I have considered the possibility. That's my job.'

'And having done your job you've come up with a number of inconsistencies. I can see that a mile off. You'd almost bet it wasn't suicide, wouldn't you?'

'I'm not a betting man,' Rillett said.

'Well, I've been around a long time and I know the pattern in suicide cases. Right from the word go I had a feeling that some things didn't fit. It's been worrying me . . . although I couldn't say why.'

'Not every case follows the same pattern.'

'Maybe not,' Quinn said. 'Let's see what the differences are in this case. Judging by the amount of gas in the hall and elsewhere in the flat I'd guess there were no towels or

rugs or anything like that stuffed under the kitchen door, were there?'
'No.'
'In fact, a reasonable guess would be that the kitchen door wasn't even shut . . . was it?'
'No, you're right.'
'Then she couldn't have pinned one of those warning notes such as "Beware Gas" outside the door . . . eh?'
'That's right, too.'
'Any farewell letter?'
Once again, Superintendent Rillett said, 'No.'
With an even more sombre light in his eyes, he added, 'I may as well tell you there was neither an eiderdown nor a layer of cushions on the kitchen floor to make her comfortable. One cushion supported her head just inside the oven.'
A feeling of compassion touched Quinn again. Death itself was not so tragic. The tragedy was that this woman might have abandoned life because she had no one to whom she could turn in her utter loneliness.
He said, 'Except for that one cushion all the classic preparations for suicide are missing. Kind of fishy, isn't it?'
'No, I wouldn't say that,' Rillett said. 'I've known cases where people have gassed themselves without going through the usual routine. There are no rules in this sort of affair. You can't expect rational behaviour from a woman who's decided to take her own life. It's not exactly the action of a sane person, is it?'
Quinn said, 'I've got my own ideas on that subject. Mind if I ask you another couple of questions?'
'Not at all—providing the answers aren't for publication.'
'That goes without saying. How long had she been dead when they got her to the hospital?'
'Within the hour . . . loosely speaking.'
'Establishing time of death—when?'
'About three o'clock. Could have been even earlier, of course.' Once more the superintendent showed that hint of faint amusement.

'How long do they think it would've taken her to die from the effects of the gas in conjunction with the sleeping pills?'

'Difficult to say. Maybe less than fifteen minutes, maybe as much as half an hour. Depends on the concentration of gas she inhaled.'

Quinn did some mental arithmetic. Then he said, 'Say she was dead by three o'clock. And say it took her half an hour to die. Now subtract twenty minutes for the sleeping pills to take effect. That should give us the time when the whole thing was set in motion.'

'Ten minutes past two,' Rillett said.

'And Heskett says he left here about two-fifteen.'

'Precisely so. Now you can see why I wanted to know what time you arrived at Denholme Court.'

'Does it matter whether I saw him or not? On the evidence of his own statement he could've done it.'

'What he told Sergeant Langdon isn't evidence. A man can alter his statement after he's thought it over. But if you had seen him leaving here . . .'

'I didn't,' Quinn said. 'So I can't say I did. While I was loitering at the corner, Heskett could've left by the rear door and been going through the gardens on his way to the garages.'

'Or he might've gone before you arrived. You aren't sure what time it was . . . and I can't make a liar of him for the sake of ten minutes.'

'Which means he could have given her a glass of doped whisky and then laid her on the kitchen floor with her head in the oven. After he'd turned on the gas taps he had only to walk out and let nature do the rest.'

Quinn rummaged through his pockets, one by one, and sighed. As he began searching again, he added, 'How to murder your wife and get away with it . . . in three easy lessons. You wouldn't happen to have a cigarette, would you? I must've left mine at the office.'

Superintendent Rillett said, 'You're unlucky. I don't smoke. Gave it up. You should do the same.'

'There are lots of things I should do ... or not do. At this stage of my life all I've decided is that I can do without advice but not cigarettes. Now where was I?'

'You were alleging, without a shred of evidence, that Mr Heskett murdered his wife.'

'Ah, yes. Well, why not?'

'There's the question of motive, for one thing.'

'That's no problem. She charged him with being Pauline's lover ... maybe even suggested he'd killed his mistress. He says himself he didn't often come home for lunch. I think his wife wanted to see him so they could have a showdown.'

Rillett nodded but there was no sign of agreement in his eyes. He said, 'Assuming that Heskett was Mrs Pauline Davey's lover, why would he want to get rid of her?'

'Could be any one of several reasons. For instance, she might've been getting serious ... and by this time he'd had enough of her.'

'So what? Nothing to stop him ending the affair. On the basis of your own theory, a man who's prepared to kill twice isn't the type to be afraid of a divorce suit. He wouldn't care if Mrs Davey told her husband or Mrs Heskett or both of them.'

Quinn said, 'You've got a habit I don't like. You keep putting up logical objections to my illogical ideas. So here's my last throw. Have you checked the whisky glass for fingerprints?'

'But of course. And those we found had been made by Mrs Davey herself. No trace of any prints but hers. Satisfied?'

'Not quite. Until you can prove somebody else was Pauline's lover I'll keep my money on Mister Heskett.'

Rillett asked, 'What have you got against the man?'

'Nothing personal. It's coincidence that I don't like. The Hesketts and the Daveys have been friends and neighbours: there's a suspicion that Heskett and Pauline Davey were on more than friendly terms: last Saturday afternoon Pauline is found murdered: this afternoon—less than forty-eight hours later—Mrs Heskett is found with her head in the gas oven: this afternoon her husband lunched with her although he himself says he rarely came home to lunch.'

Quinn finished counting on his fingers. He asked, 'Would you call that coincidence or would you call it coincidence?'

'It adds up all right,' Rillett said. 'The only trouble is that we get the wrong answer.'

'Maybe because we're using the wrong formula. Don't forget we wouldn't have been able to work out such an accurate time-table if somebody hadn't pushed a leaflet through that letter-box while I was snooping around. If the front door of 2C and the letter-box flap are pretty tight fitting I might never have detected the smell of gas. And if I hadn't . . .'

'The time of death couldn't have been established so closely,' Rillett said.

He hummed a few tuneless notes under his breath while he stared with empty eyes at a picture on the wall of the dining-annexe. Then he asked, 'Ever met Neil Heskett?'

'No. I've been told he's an architect and Pauline Davey was seen on one occasion making eyes at him . . . but apart from that bit of gossip I know nothing about the fellow.'

'Any idea what he looks like?'

'Not a clue. I imagine he's quite personable but otherwise—'

'Then how do you know you didn't see him leaving here?'

Quinn began feeling in his raincoat pockets again. He said, 'If I let you in on a secret can we go and have that pint you promised me?'

'By all means.'

'Well, it's like this. I know I didn't see Heskett because, as it just so happens, I didn't see anybody coming or going when I arrived at Denholme Court. Didn't you think of that?'

Rillett said, 'Yes. But I thought I'd better ask all the same. And I've also thought of something else that apparently hasn't entered your head because you've been so busy building up a case against Heskett.'

'What's the something else?'

'It's based on part of your theory that Heskett and Pauline Davey had been having an affair.'

'Yes?'

'Oh, nothing much.' Rillett's half-smile lasted only a moment. 'Let's go and have that pint you're gasping for. When you've quenched your thirst, perhaps you'll know what I have in mind.'

'Perhaps I won't,' Quinn said. 'Don't be mean. I'm not as clever as you are.'

'All right. Here's an idea to ponder over. Hasn't it struck you that Pauline Davey must've been killed by somebody who was either crazy or in a frantic rage?'

'Yes, it has. From what I understand, she was stabbed again and again. The doctor's evidence at the inquest this morning didn't leave much doubt that one or two of the wounds would have been fatal on their own. She didn't need to be butchered like she was.'

'Exactly my point. Neil Heskett could've disposed of her without getting into a frenzy. A nylon stocking round her neck would have been quieter, more certain and less messy. Right?'

Quinn said, 'I wouldn't argue with that.'

'Then you'll agree that the same objection applies to her husband. He might well have been furious but why should he risk getting blood all over himself when he knew your friend Piper was arriving at half-past five?'

'True. I'm with you so far.'

'Right. Now I'll quote you. Didn't you suggest that Mrs Heskett might have found out what her husband was up to?'

With a look of awareness sharpening his thin features, Quinn said, 'I did . . . indeed, I did. And I think, Superintendent, that you've hit on the answer. If she was keeping watch on him and waited until he left 2C and went back into his own flat—'

'She could've gone visiting her neighbour,' Rillett said. 'I would imagine she hated Pauline enough to treat her pretty horribly.'

'And maybe today she couldn't keep it to herself any longer so she asked her husband to come home and confessed the whole thing to him. Wonder if he threatened to tell the police?'

Superintendent Rillett said, 'Only way to find out is to ask him. But one thing I know. Mrs Heskett could've had every reason to commit suicide.'

CHAPTER VIII

THE gaming room of the Armada Casino was ornately appointed—gilt chandeliers and gilt-framed mirrors, a crimson-and-gold décor enhancing the green baize of the tables. Golden men-of-war, frigates and galleons were woven into the carpets and hangings. The farthest part of the long spacious room was railed off as a restaurant on a split-level section of the main floor.

It was almost five o'clock when Piper arrived. Someone told him he would find Mr Tew in his office.

'... It's over there on the right. Says *MANAGER* on the door.'

Tew's office was barely large enough to accommodate a massive safe, two desks, a filing cabinet and several chairs. It had no window and an extraction fan provided the only ventilation. A single light had been switched on over the desk where Tew was working.

He had a craggy face, deep-set eyes, a nose that looked as though at one time it had been broken. By contrast his smile was pleasant and he had the voice of a man of education.

Piper introduced himself and explained that he was acting for Mr Julian Davey. '... I suppose you've heard what happened to his wife?'

In a tone that carefully enunciated each word, Tew said, 'Someone told me about it over the week-end. Nasty business.'

With scarcely a pause, he asked, 'Why should Mr Davey require your services?'

'Because of the allegation that his wife had a lover. Unless and until the police find out who killed her, he'll be in a rather embarrassing situation.'

'Embarrassing—' Tew's rugged face was almost naive—'can have several meanings.'

'I mean he could have learned of his wife's relationship with this other man.'

'Possibly. But I am sure that is not all you mean.'

'Frankly, no. Davey is afraid people will believe he had a motive for the murder of his wife.'

Tew said, 'I'll say this much for you, Mr Piper. You are certainly blunt.'

'It would serve no purpose to be otherwise,' Piper said. 'I can't expect your help if I go beating about the bush.'

'That's what puzzles me. How can I help you?'

'By talking about Mrs Pauline Davey and the people she associated with when she visited your casino.'

'Unfortunately—' there was a hint of apology in Tew's rounded voice—'I make it a practice never to discuss our members or their guests.'

Piper said, 'I can well appreciate that . . . but it shouldn't stand in your way. Whatever you tell me won't do Mrs Davey any harm now she's dead.'

'But I don't know anything about her private life. And that's obviously what you're interested in. She was just someone who played the wheel same as perhaps a thousand other people.'

'There was one difference in her case,' Piper said. 'Friday night she left here very late. Saturday afternoon she got stabbed to death. Wouldn't you say that entitles you to break your normal practice?'

With his chin in his hand Tew pondered for a while. Then he said, 'I think my best course will be to play it by ear and see how we get on. At the moment I feel you haven't served Mr Davey's interests by coming to see me . . . but I won't presume to teach you your business. Now go ahead.'

Piper said, 'Thank you. First of all, did Mrs Davey spend her time with anyone in particular?'

'No, I wouldn't say so. Of course, I'm in my office a lot but I know most of our regular patrons and the friends they meet here.'

'Did she have many friends?'

'As far as I know—yes. She was an attractive woman and people liked her.'

'An attractive woman unaccompanied,' Piper said.

'Nothing unusual in that.' Tew was still pleasant and disarming. 'Lady members are not obliged to come with an escort. We vet every applicant before membership is granted to ensure impeccable behaviour.'

'Of course. I'm not suggesting Mrs Davey behaved in any way that was questionable. But she wasn't often accompanied by her husband . . . and so she must've attracted a certain amount of male attention.'

'Only a certain amount. Most men come here to take their chance at the tables—not to dilly-dally.'

In an off-hand voice, Tew added, 'That goes for the ladies, too.'

Piper said, 'I've no doubt. In the course of a long evening however, they must have a meal or something to drink. On these occasions, did Mrs Davey mix with any one group of people?'

'Over a period I wouldn't think so.'

'Nobody she met very often?'

'Well, if—' Tew pulled at his ear and hesitated—'if I were pressed I'd say she saw quite a lot of her neighbours at Denholme Court.'

'Which neighbours?'

'Mrs Wrexham, for one. I've also seen her in the company of Mr and Mrs Heskett. Sometimes he's been on his own and he and Mrs Davey have spent a little time together.'

'Friday night, for instance?'

'No, neither Mr nor Mrs Heskett was here on Friday. I saw Mrs Wrexham chatting with Mrs Davey but I didn't particularly notice any men around . . . and it's a man you're looking for, isn't it?'

'One special man,' Piper said.

Tew leaned back and stretched. With something behind his nicely-modulated voice that had not been there before, he asked, 'Would you mind if I put a question to you about

Mr Davey . . . in confidence?'

'Not in the least.'

'Good. It's this: what makes you so sure he didn't murder his wife?'

Piper knew it was a question that would be asked more and more frequently as time went on. And there was only one answer he could give.

He said, 'I'm not sure. I have his word for it . . . that's all. Now you tell me something. What makes you imply he may have been the person who killed her?'

In an easy voice, Tew said, 'I didn't intend it as an implication. That would be going too far. I just felt that in searching for this other man you might be on the wrong track.'

'How?'

'Well, possibly there's nothing in it but, if you'd like me to suggest an alternative approach . . .'

'I'd be grateful for any suggestion,' Piper said.

'Then, instead of concentrating on another man, think along the lines of another woman. I'd never have thought of putting it forward except for the fact that it happened on Saturday, the day his wife was murdered. As I say, it may be just a wild idea but—'

'What happened on Saturday?'

'Mr Davey came to see me. His wife had left her cigarette lighter on Friday night and she'd phoned next morning to inquire if we'd found it. In actual fact, we had.'

Tew paused. With a slight air of surprise, he asked, 'Didn't Davey mention he'd been here on Saturday?'

'No. What time did he arrive?'

'Between half-past one and two. I'd told his wife her lighter would be in my office and so he came straight to me. As it happens I was engaged . . . and that's what I've had in mind while we've been talking. Of course, I don't doubt it was a chance encounter but I still wonder what took place after they left . . .'

Piper said, 'Please go on. All this is news to me. Whom did he meet?'

'Someone by the name of Ward—Susan Ward. I was interviewing her for the post of secretary/cashier and when Davey looked in they recognized each other. From the way they spoke I gathered they were old friends. She seemed particularly glad to see him.'

'Did they leave together?'

'Yes, that's the whole point. Davey collected his wife's lighter and told this Miss Ward he'd wait until the interview was over. If she hadn't come in her own car he'd be happy to drop her wherever she was going.'

After another pause, Tew went on, 'She said that was very nice of him. So he waited.'

'How long?'

'Only a few minutes. I'd already made up my mind she was the kind of person I wanted and all we had to do was discuss the final details such as the date she could start.'

'Is she working for you now?'

'No. We arranged that she'd take up her duties a week from today.'

'And after that she and Davey left together?'

'Yes.' Tew gave Piper a long probing look. 'I suppose he was questioned about what he did and where he went on Saturday afternoon?'

'You're right. He was.'

'Wonder why he didn't tell you he'd been here and had gone off with a woman friend?'

'So do I.'

Tew said, 'If he didn't want you to know, there might just be something in it . . . don't you think?'

Something . . . or nothing. Julian Davey had perhaps not mentioned it because he had far bigger things on his mind. He and this Miss Ward had met by chance. It was no crime to give her a lift on his way to the football match.

'I doubt it,' Piper said. 'All he did was offer to drop her somewhere. Sounds quite innocent to me.'

'But you haven't heard—' Tew smiled thinly—'the interesting sequel. To start with, Miss Ward didn't need a lift.

She'd come here in her own car.'

'How do you know?'

'She hadn't wound up her driving window when she left it in our private car park. Later that afternoon one of our staff reported that whoever owned the car was just asking for it to be pinched. He'd seen her arrive just after one o'clock and he thought she should be told to lock the car if she intended to stay much longer.'

'Might not have been Miss Ward,' Piper said.

'Oh, yes, it was. He saw her going into my office.'

With a shrug, Tew added, 'I only had one woman visitor around that time. Couldn't be anybody else.'

'What did you do about the car?'

'Told him to shut the window and instruct the commissionaire to keep an eye open for prowlers. Since we didn't have a key there was nothing else we could do.'

Piper had no wish to lean over backwards but this whole story involved only one person. Miss Ward had sought Davey's company—not the other way round. Her reason might be open to question . . . but that was for her to explain.

'Some women are very absent-minded,' Piper said.

'Not to that extent.' Tew shook his head. 'The top and bottom of it is that she saw her chance to be with Davey and she wasn't going to lose it.'

'Perhaps you're right. What happened eventually to her car?'

'Well, it wasn't there when we shut up shop in the early hours of Sunday morning so she must've come back for it some time Saturday afternoon or evening. No one saw it driving off.'

'Could've been stolen.'

'Not likely. If it had she'd have been round here . . . and so would the law. We've heard nothing since she left with Davey.'

Piper wondered where they had gone and how much time they had spent in each other's company. If Davey's conscience was clean he should be willing to talk about it freely.

'I'd like to hear more about Miss Ward,' Piper said. 'What sort of person is she?'

'Quite pretty and speaks well. Twenty-nine or thirty. Was married but divorced her husband a month ago. That's why she wanted this job. Used to be in a similar position and is undoubtedly very efficient.'

Tew gave Piper another long look and asked, 'Are you thinking of calling on her?'

'It might be an idea . . . if you don't mind giving me her address.'

'I don't mind at all. I'm sure you'll be discreet.'

'Of course. I won't even tell her I've spoken to you.'

'Somehow—' Tew shrugged again—'I've a feeling it won't really matter what you say. My hunch is that Miss Susan Ward will be the one that got away.'

'You think she won't turn up for work next Monday?'

'I'll lay you better odds than you'll get at any of the tables,' Tew said. 'After what happened to Mrs Pauline Davey it's a safe bet.'

His hard bony face creased in a grin as he added, 'If it weren't, I wouldn't have told you all about Miss Ward and how she met an old friend right here in my office.'

He wrote out the address and pushed it across his desk. Then he asked, 'Like to do me a small favour in return for all the information?'

'If I can I'll be only too pleased.'

'Oh, you certainly can. Just keep my name out of this affair from now on. It isn't good for business to have the Armada linked with a *cause célèbre*. Murder is the sort of publicity we can do without.'

Piper said, 'I'll do my best . . .'

He went back to his office and rang Susan Ward's number. There was no reply.

When he tried again at six o'clock the bell rang and

rang without response. A third attempt met with no more success. At ten past six he went home.

Jane had left a note: *Forgot to mention dental appointment 5.45. If you're starving, don't wait for me. Casserole in oven. Help yourself.*

His solitary meal reminded him like an old wound of the years he wanted to forget. Even washing up after he had eaten was all too familiar. If he had known he would have had a meal in town.

An inner voice told him he was being childish. No man was entitled to feel sorry for himself because he had to eat alone once in a while. Jane must never know. It was just plain silly . . .

At seven o'clock he rang Susan Ward's number again. This time a woman answered. She had a pleasing voice with no particular accent.

He said, 'My name's Piper—John Piper. I understand you're a friend of Mr Julian Davey?'

Her hesitation lasted only long enough to be noticeable. With a trace of caution, she said, 'Yes, I know Mr Davey. Is anything wrong?'

'No, he's all right. But I suppose you've heard about his wife.'

'Heard what?'

The question was enough in itself. If Miss Ward needed to lie, she must have good reason for lying. Now she was committed.

Piper said, 'It was in all this morning's papers.'

'I haven't taken more than a glance at the paper today. What's happened to Mrs Davey?'

'She's dead. I thought you would've known.'

'No . . . I didn't. It's quite some time since I met either Mr Davey or his wife . . . but I'm terribly sorry to hear it.'

Susan Ward should have stopped there. Instead, she added, 'The poor man must be very upset.'

'That's putting it mildly,' Piper said.

The phone was silent as if she were waiting for him to go on. When she could wait no longer, she asked, 'Did you just want to tell me about Mrs Davey . . . or was there something else?'

'There is something else,' Piper said. 'I'd like to have a talk with you, preferably right now.'

'I don't know what you mean.' Her voice had sharpened. 'Why should you want to talk to me?'

He was afraid of saying too much but the risk had to be taken. He said, 'Because the police are checking Julian Davey's movements on Saturday afternoon. Very soon he'll need to produce an alibi for the time his wife was murdered.'

Now it was Piper's turn to wait. After a long time, she asked, 'Why come to me? What makes you think I know where he was?'

'I don't have to think. You were seen with Davey in his car at two o'clock that day. If you try to deny it I'll hand my information over to the police.'

She made two false starts before she said, 'I've done nothing wrong, so if the idea is to blackmail me—'

'It isn't,' Piper said. 'Mr Davey has employed me to protect his interests and that's where you may be able to help. But we can't afford any delay. If he's innocent of what they suspect, he has already behaved very foolishly. Between us, you and I may get him out of trouble—with luck and if we don't waste any time. I must see you right away.'

Susan Ward took ten seconds to make up her mind. Then she said, 'All right. I had an engagement . . . but I'll cancel it.'

The phone rang as Piper was leaving. Quinn said, 'I don't know how you got on at the Armada Casino but I've been where the action is—to coin a phrase. Not that I'd like to repeat the experience . . . as the curate said on his wedding night. I'd still have a nasty taste in my mouth if Superintendent Rillett hadn't pushed the boat out at a very nice place—'

'You'll have to cut it short,' Piper said. 'I've a date with

a young lady and I don't want to keep her waiting.'
'Which young lady—Jane? And don't say that's no lady, that's my wife, because if you do—'
'It isn't Jane. It's a Miss Susan Ward who lives at Queen's Park and who's expecting me very shortly.'
'Anything to do with our present activities?'
'Yes. She's a friend of Julian Davey. They met on Saturday when he called in at the casino . . .'

Quinn coughed once or twice while he listened but for the most part he was unusually quiet. At the end, he said, 'Well, well, whadaya know? It's beginning to look as if Mister Davey never went to the match, after all. If he didn't, he may have to account for his movements not only on Saturday but this afternoon, as well.'

'Why?'

'Because this afternoon Mrs Heskett joined her friend and neighbour, Pauline Davey, in the Promised Land. There was some doubt as to whether she'd done it herself or someone had done it to her but now . . .'

His story was short and to the point. For once he avoided any digression, for once he used the language of his daily column.

A pattern began to form in Piper's mind. At its core he kept glimpsing that momentary picture of Julian Davey passing the door with a laden tea-tray.

There could be only one conclusion. It permitted no escape. Davey's fate might well depend on how much Susan Ward could be trusted.

Piper said, 'If it wasn't suicide, why should Davey want to get rid of Mrs Heskett? She'd been betrayed as much as he had . . . assuming her husband was Pauline Davey's lover. What harm had Mrs Heskett done?'

'I could make a guess,' Quinn said. 'No proof, of course. Nobody'll ever be able to prove a thing now she's dead . . .'

'Never mind the proof. What's your guess?'

'She must've seen him return home on Saturday afternoon some time before half-past five. Might even have seen him go out again and return later with you. If she told him what she saw that day there was only one thing he could do ... unless he liked the idea of a long stretch.'

'What if Susan Ward is willing to swear he was with her until after five o'clock and couldn't have got back before he met me?'

'Then Mister Julian Davey stands every chance of getting away with murder,' Quinn said.

CHAPTER IX

HUBERT DRIVE consisted of solid old houses overlooking Birdcage Green—a grass rectangle surrounded by trees fenced in on all four sides. Many of the houses had been converted to flats.

Number 16 faced the gate to the miniature park. In a row of letter-boxes Piper found Susan Ward's name. She lived on the top floor.

He saw no one as he climbed the stairs. When he was passing the second floor he could faintly hear the music of a radio but it was too far away to let him recognize the melody.

On his way up the last flight of stairs, memory recaptured those moments on Saturday afternoon when Julian Davey carried a tea tray into his wife's bedroom—moments threaded together by a phrase from a song of long ago. Once again the voice crooned softly in Piper's mind.

'. . . *You promised that you'd forget me not, but you forgot to remember.*'

He had not known then that Pauline Davey was dead, that his visit to Denholme Court would be the prelude to tragedy. Now Mrs Heskett—friend and neighbour—had also died.

Friendship had linked them together in life but it must be more than just friendly association that now bound them for all time in death. Mrs Heskett had not committed suicide because she was overwrought with grief. To believe otherwise was to exaggerate the bonds of friendship.

The tune of that old song still ran through his head as he stopped outside Susan Ward's flat. He had to make a conscious effort to get rid of it before he knocked at the door.

She was a slim, fine-boned woman with small features, grey eyes and red-brown hair. Her colouring and her look of serenity reminded him of a François Clouet miniature.

He said, 'Miss Ward?'

'Yes. You must be Mr Piper. Please come in.'

Her voice was even more pleasing than it had sounded on the phone. He began to wonder why her husband had ever given her grounds for divorce.

Whatever uneasiness she might have felt an hour before had gone. Now her manner was that of someone with the power to dispense favours.

She led the way into a room tastefully furnished and lit by two shaded panel lights. When she had asked him to take a seat she moved a little farther away and stood looking down at him, her hands folded placidly in front of her.

Then in a small grave voice, she said, 'You are not quite what I expected.'

Piper asked, 'What did you expect, Miss Ward?'

'Well, for one thing, you look like a policeman.'

'So I have often been told.'

'Are you, or have you ever been, connected with the police?'

'No. But does it matter what I am? The question is what you are, Miss Ward.'

'I don't understand.' She was unmoved, unafraid. 'Please be good enough to explain.'

'You should understand,' Piper said. 'And I think you do. But, if it will save time, this is the position. Julian Davey has told the police he went to a football match at Highbury on Saturday afternoon. I have reason to believe he did no such thing. According to my information he spent the afternoon with you.'

Her eyes clung to Piper's face. In the same grave voice, she asked, 'And if he did?'

'Then you may be the only person who can get him out of trouble. As I mentioned on the phone he may need an alibi, and need one very badly. The fact that you denied being with him doesn't say much for his chances.'

With just a trace of indignation, Susan Ward said, 'You have no right saying a thing like that.'

'I've got every right. He's paying me to keep him from

landing in an awkward situation. If you have any regard at all for Julian Davey you'll co-operate with me. It costs you nothing . . . and it's the least you can do for a friend.'

'I don't need you to teach me my duty. How do I know you are acting for Mr Davey?'

'Give him a ring,' Piper said.

She clasped and unclasped her fingers several times while her eyes travelled absently here and there. When they settled on Piper again, she asked, 'Why should the police suspect he killed his wife? What motive could he have had?'

Piper said, 'Look, Miss Ward, don't treat me like a child. I've an idea—just an idea—that Davey has spoken to you since the week-end. You know his wife had a lover. You know as much as I do . . . and more. So either you talk to me or you talk to the police. The choice is yours.'

'That sounds—' her composure was wearing thin—'very much like an ultimatum. You threatened the same thing on the phone. I'm beginning to suspect that you are not so concerned for Mr Davey's welfare as you would have me believe.'

'What you believe is your own affair. I'm only interested in the truth . . . because the truth can't harm Julian Davey if he's innocent. If he isn't, I'm not going to cover up for him. The question is—are you?'

She hesitated but only for a few seconds. The look in her steady grey eyes told him she had reached a decision.

With a slight thawing of the shell that had surrounded her, she said, 'It would do no good even if I did it to protect him. Besides there's no need for me to lie. I can honestly account for his movements. He was with me for the best part of Saturday afternoon.'

'Where?'

'Well, for a start, he asked me if I'd had lunch. When I told him I'd intended to eat after my appointment at the Armada Casino, he insisted on taking me to a steak bar he knew.'

She moistened her lips and asked, 'You knew, of course, we met at the casino?'

'Yes, I knew,' Piper said.

'It was quite by chance. I hadn't seen Julian for almost three years and he was the last person I'd expected to meet. Maybe I shouldn't have let him take me to lunch but I was in the mood for pleasant company . . .'

Her even voice tailed off. Piper said, 'Especially Julian Davey's company.'

'Yes, why not?' She had a look in her eyes of transparent honesty. 'I've always liked Julian. I knew him long before I got married.'

'Was he married then?'

'No, but—' for the first time Piper saw what lay in her thoughts—'but that's another story. It was all so long ago.'

'The story of two people who made a mistake,' Piper said.

Regret, and something more than regret, clouded her eyes. She said, 'I've gone too far to hold anything back now. I must trust you. I've no alternative.'

Piper said, 'I've already told you, Miss Ward, that if Davey had no hand in the death of his wife he has nothing to fear from me. It's not a question of the fee I'm being paid. Providing he's innocent, I won't betray your trust.'

'No . . . no, I don't think you will.' A wistful smile touched her lips. 'I haven't really anything to hide. If I hadn't taken so long to make up my mind I'd have married Julian . . . and perhaps none of this would've happened. In a sense, it could be my fault.'

'Why do you say that?'

'Well, I've always believed our lives follow a pattern. It isn't the only one but it's the one that governs us from stage to stage according to decisions we make at certain critical moments. They are the key pieces of the pattern. Change any one of them and you change the whole course of your life.'

'A variable destiny,' Piper said.

'Yes, if you like. But, in this case, my destiny was linked with Pauline Davey. If I had married Julian she wouldn't have become his wife. Last Saturday she wouldn't have been alone in her flat . . .'

Susan Ward ended with a little sigh. Then she added, 'Maybe you think I'm being silly but that's how I feel. If she hadn't been Julian's wife she wouldn't be dead.'

Piper said, 'I don't think you're silly. But if you should ever be questioned by the police, take my advice and don't pursue that trend of thought. They may take it the wrong way.'

'I didn't mean he—' She shied away from what must follow.

'No, of course you didn't. I know what you meant. Now do you feel inclined to answer a few more questions?'

Her body seemed to relax and her small, delicate face became placid again. She said, 'If it's going to help Julian, ask me anything you wish.'

'All right. Did he have lunch with you?'

'Only an omelette and coffee. He said he'd had a bite to eat before he left home.'

'What did you do after lunch?'

'We sat for a while over a drink and talked. Just talked. It had been such a long time since—' she gave Piper another wistful smile—'since we last met.'

'How long did you sit talking?'

'Until about three o'clock.'

'Had he told you he was supposed to be going to Highbury?'

'Only after it was too late. He'd forgotten all about the match.'

After a slight pause, she added, 'Or so he said.' Her mouth was as demure as the miniature that Piper remembered.

'Where did you go when you left the steak bar?'

'He ran me home.'

'When you got here did he come upstairs?'

Susan Ward drew in a deep breath and let it out slowly. She said, 'No, Mr Piper, it wasn't like that at all. Whatever you may be thinking, we didn't go to bed.'

'I had to know,' Piper said. 'It could be important.'

'If you say so. As a matter of fact we took a stroll in Birdcage Green and then sat on a bench enjoying the sunshine. If you remember, it was a very nice afternoon.'

'How long were you there?'

'Perhaps an hour. I'm not sure.'

Piper roughly calculated the various elements of time. He said, 'Let's suppose you arrived here between three-fifteen and three-thirty. Then you and Davey spent approximately an hour in Birdcage Green. That would make it, say, half-past four. Of course, I'm assuming the steak bar wasn't far from the Armada Casino?'

'No . . . not very far. It's in the Finchley Road.'

'That being so, my estimate must be reasonably close. Would you agree, therefore, that he left you some time around four-thirty?'

Uncertainty put little lines at the corners of her eyes. She said, 'I couldn't be sure. I wasn't paying any attention to the time. It might've been later than that.'

'How much later . . . at a maximum?'

'I've told you I'm not sure. You can't expect a precise answer if I don't know.'

'The police will expect an answer,' Piper said. 'Julian Davey arrived at Denholme Court, where he lives, at half-past five. No matter how bad traffic conditions were on Saturday afternoon, he couldn't have taken an hour to do the journey from Queen's Park to Cornstalk Avenue, Hampstead.'

Susan Ward said, 'Then it must've been near five o'clock when he left me.' Her eyes told Piper she had no faith in her own suggestion.

When he just went on looking at her, she added, 'Nothing will ever convince me he would've dreamed of harming his wife. The idea that he went home and killed her is absolutely absurd.'

'Absurd it may be. But, if he didn't go straight home, where did he go? Furthermore, why did he lie by saying he'd been to the match at Highbury?'

'I don't know.' She shook her head and repeated, 'I don't know.'

Piper said, 'Very well. Just another couple of things I'd like to clear up. When he was bringing you back here did you tell him you hadn't needed a lift, that you'd driven to the Armada in your own car?'

She looked momentarily surprised. Then she said, 'I won't ask how you knew that.'

'You may if you want. But I'd rather you answered my question. Did you tell Davey you'd accepted his offer of a lift because you wanted to renew an old association?'

With no change of tone, she said, 'I hadn't any such thought. It just seemed like a pleasant interlude with someone I liked after all the not-so-pleasant things that have been happening to me recently. I suppose you know I divorced my husband?'

'Yes. And I'm sorry if I phrased my question badly. When did you pick up your car from the casino?'

'Saturday evening.'

'Have you been in touch with Julian Davey since that afternoon?'

'No.'

'Has he been in touch with you—by phone or otherwise?'

Without any hesitation, she said, 'No. Perhaps you can't understand it but I don't mean anything to him. I'm just somebody he once knew. I happened along on Saturday as an alternative to a football match that he wasn't especially keen on. Whether you believe me or not, I can assure you I'll never see him again.'

'Although both of you are now free to take up where you left off when he married the wrong woman and you married the wrong man?'

'Nothing we discussed—' Susan Ward was still calm and self-possessed—'gave me the slightest impression that he'd married the wrong woman.'

'Any mention that he wasn't happy with his wife?'

'No, none at all.'

'Or that he suspected she was having an affair?'

'No.'

In a steady voice, Susan Ward added, 'I don't know of any reason he could've had to kill his wife ... and I don't believe he did kill her. It was foolish of him to say he'd gone to a football match when he'd actually been with me, but that doesn't make him a criminal.'

'Foolish is the wrong word,' Piper said. 'It puts you in a false position.'

'Why should it?'

'Because now the police may think he didn't say where he'd really been for only one reason. He was afraid of disclosing his relationship with you.'

'His relationship with me began and ended on Saturday afternoon. I'll go on saying that because it's the truth.'

'All right, no need to fight with me. For Davey's sake I just wish we could account for that half-hour between four-thirty and five o'clock.'

She looked at Piper wide-eyed. In an innocent voice, she said, 'Oh, but we can. While you were talking to me, I remembered. When I came upstairs after he'd driven away it was just after five.'

Piper collected his hat from the floor beside his chair. As he stood up, he asked, 'Would you be willing to swear to that on oath if it should ever be necessary.'

'Yes, of course.'

'You're not afraid of committing perjury?'

Susan Ward said, 'I've nothing to be afraid of if I say it was five o'clock ... to the best of my knowledge.'

'In view of what I know, you could be asking for trouble, Miss Ward. Aren't you forgetting you told me it was about half-past four?'

'Did I?' Her delicate features had suddenly hardened. 'Isn't there something you're forgetting? Aren't you supposed to be acting in Julian Davey's interests?'

'Not if it means conspiring with you so that he escapes a charge of murder,' Piper said.

As though she had not heard him, as though he no longer existed, she stood quite still, her eyes empty of all feeling. When he left her she made no move to see him to the door.

She had not stirred by the time he went out. Before he pulled the door shut he paused for a moment and listened. There was no sound inside the flat, no sound anywhere except the muted radio so far away that its music was only scattered notes without the sequence of a melody.

On his way downstairs he could still see the look of emptiness in Susan Ward's eyes. She had made her decision. For her there was no going back. To save Julian Davey she would lie, whatever the cost.

CHAPTER X

SHORTLY before eight o'clock he arrived at Denholme Court. The moon was up—a misty harvest moon in a sky still luminous with the afterglow of sunset. There was a hint of frost in the air and an acrid smell of burning leaves.

The lift was on an upper floor. Instead of waiting he used the stairs.

When he got to the first landing he could hear voices in a nearby flat—raised voices like those of people quarrelling. One of them sounded vaguely familiar.

He rang the bell of flat 2A and stood listening to the musical chime fading into silence. No one answered when he pressed the bell-push again . . . and again.

By that time he had recognized one of the voices and he knew why there was no reply from Davey's flat. After a moment's thought he rapped on the door of 2C.

The disputing voices broke off. Except for the sound of a passing car everything was quiet.

When nothing happened he knocked again. As he was about to try a third time the door opened.

A man in a cream shirt asked, 'Yes?'

His collar was undone, his sleeves rolled up, his matching tie unfastened. The ends hung down unevenly.

He was a good-looking man of athletic build and well-cut features who could have been either side of forty. He looked angry.

Piper said, 'Mr Heskett?'

'Yes. Can I help you?' His tone was surly to the point of rudeness.

'Maybe later,' Piper said. 'Right now I'd like to speak to Mr Davey. He's with you, isn't he?'

'What you'd like or not like—' Heskett began to close the door—'doesn't mean a damn' thing to me. This is my home—not Piccadilly Circus. If you want Davey you can wait where you are until he leaves. In my opinion that won't be long.'

Piper stuck his foot in the door. He said, 'Your opinion doesn't mean a damn' thing to me, Mr Heskett. I don't intend to wait.'

A rush of temper flared in Heskett's face. He said, 'If you don't get your foot out of there I'll teach you a—'

'You'll teach me nothing. Go and tell Davey I've got some bad news for him. If he isn't interested, the police will be. And while they're here they may ask you just how friendly you were with the late Pauline Davey.'

Heskett's temper burned itself out rapidly. In a changed voice, he asked, 'Who are you?'

'My name's Piper. Your friend Davey knows me. It could save trouble—maybe for both of you—if you were to invite me in.'

A long moment went by while Heskett stood clenching and unclenching his hands. Then he stepped back from the door. His face was still forbidding.

He said, 'All right. I'll listen to what you have to say...'

Julian Davey was in the kitchen. He could scarcely have failed to hear the conversation on the landing.

His blond hair was ruffled, his eyes nervous. He said, 'I've been expecting you to phone me.' It sounded as though he could find no other remark to make.

'This is much better than talking on the phone,' Piper said. 'I'll be able to kill two birds with the one stone. However, if you were in the middle of a friendly discussion don't let me stop you. I'm in no particular hurry.'

Behind him, Heskett said, 'It wasn't a discussion, friendly or otherwise. It was an indictment.'

He came round in front of Piper and went on, 'Whatever you have to do with this business, I'm glad you've come. When you've said your little piece you can take this—' he pointed a long forefinger at Davey—'this lunatic away and see he doesn't bother me again. He's crazy.'

Julian Davey said, 'Oh, no, I'm not—not now. But I have been without knowing it. Now that I've added up all the apparent trifles. I realize I must've been blind. For months, you and Pauline—'

'That's a damned lie! There was nothing between your wife and me. If she was playing around it was with some other man. After what's happened to Deborah you might've had the decency to keep your dirty suspicions to yourself. The poor girl is hardly cold . . .' Heskett put a hand over his eyes and turned to face the wall.

'Don't be a bloody hypocrite! Deborah committed suicide because she found out that Pauline had been your mistress. It was you who went to bed with her on Saturday afternoon. What else you did—'

As though something had caught in his throat, Davey stopped. His face seemed to have gone numb.

Slowly and jerkily Heskett swivelled round a little at a time until they were staring at each other. Piper had the feeling they had forgotten he was there.

Once they had been friends. Now they were like two dogs fighting over a bone.

It was a dried-up bone of no worth to either of them. They had lost everything that should have given purpose to their lives. The tangled knots of existence had been ripped apart by the events of one afternoon.

Perhaps they had not known on Saturday morning how soon the world would become a different place. Yet perhaps one of them had chosen that day to rid himself of a burden . . . or an object of hate. Perhaps . . . So much depended on which of them had the stronger motive to kill.

In that moment, Piper hardly cared. It was unimportant whether Pauline Davey had been more sinned against than sinning.

Her death had set off a chain-reaction. Now another woman was dead. Reason or motive could never alter what had happened. Regret had no power to turn back the clock. Two women had died . . .

Heskett said with difficulty, 'I thought you must be out of your mind. Now I know it. Are you mad enough to suggest that I killed Pauline?'

When he had got rid of the lump in his throat, Julian Davey asked, 'Why not? Why couldn't it have been you? Isn't it more likely to have been you than me?'

Doubt showed in Heskett's eyes. He said, 'Now you're talking complete nonsense. Who'd be fool enough to think you had done it?'

'The police . . . to start with.'

'In the name of sanity, why?'

'They think I must've found out that Pauline was carrying on with you.'

'There was nothing to find out,' Heskett said.

He looked at Piper and asked, 'Where do you come into all this?'

'I've been retained by Mr Davey to ferret out the truth,' Piper said. 'From what I've heard in the past couple of minutes we'll never get anywhere near it unless both of you stop lying. Can't you see it doesn't matter any more, that you don't need to keep up the pretence?'

Davey opened his mouth and then decided to say nothing. Heskett made a grumbling sound that had no more meaning than the withdrawn look on his face.

After a long silence, Davey said, 'He's right. It's time we put our cards on the table, if only to stay out of trouble.'

He gave Heskett a tired look and added, 'You may as well know I don't care, I don't care at all, what you and Pauline were to each other. It's too late for me to break my heart over a thing like that. She's dead. Whatever she did to me doesn't matter now. When I think of the way she died I can't even hate her.'

'And me?' Heskett seemed to dredge the question up from a great depth. 'What do you feel about me?'

In a wooden voice, Davey said, 'You're a cheat and a liar . . . that's what you are, Neil. You betrayed our friendship. If your mistress hadn't already paid a horrible price for what the two of you did to me, I think I'd want to kill you.'

'The way you talk—'

'That's right. That's all it is—talk. I've no reason to kill you. The reason ceased to exist when my wife died. If you murdered her you'll pay in a different currency. And then the account will be settled.'

Heskett said huskily, 'I didn't harm her at all. I could never have harmed her. She was a wonderful person . . . I've never met anyone like her. What made me behave as I did is something I won't even try to explain. You can despise me all you want . . . I'm not sorry for what I did.'

With a tremor in his hands Davey walked over to the sink and stood there with his back turned. As the moments passed his whole body began to tremble.

Then he suddenly went still. Heskett had no more to say. Piper watched and waited.

At last, Davey turned. In a deflated voice, he said, 'I despise you for what you are—not what you did. You can't be held entirely responsible for that. Pauline was as much to blame, perhaps—' his voice was fading as though he had run out of breath—'perhaps even more.'

Piper asked, 'Did you ever guess she was being unfaithful?'

Like a man bringing his mind back from a long way off, Davey said, 'No, never. I can hardly believe it now . . . although I know it's true.'

In sudden violence he took a step towards Heskett and asked, 'Isn't it, Neil? Isn't it true that you went to bed with my wife last Saturday afternoon?'

Heskett said, 'Yes . . . yes, dammit, it's true! Are you satisfied now? Are you enjoying your martyrdom? Maybe if you'd been more of a man, Pauline wouldn't have needed to—'

He went back and almost toppled over as Davey struck him a swinging blow to the face—an open-handed blow that sounded like the bursting of a paper bag. It seemed to cause Heskett more surprise than pain.

As he felt his jaw, he said, 'You know, I didn't think you had it in you. I deserved that. If you'd like to have another go it's all right with me.'

'You can go to hell,' Davey said.

'Sooner or later I've no doubt I will. But at the moment

I'm not going anywhere. I live here. If you and your friend have finished you can get out.'

Piper said, 'He may have finished but I haven't. Someone murdered Pauline Davey. That can't be disposed of by a smack in the face. And there's the death of your own wife in circumstances which demand some explanation.'

'Why should I explain to you?'

'Either to me or the police. They'll have to be told that you and Mrs Davey were lovers. Once they know that, you'll be questioned on what exactly took place here in this flat when you came home at lunchtime today. By telling me first you'll be able to make your story more plausible when the time comes to tell them.'

Without any rancour, Heskett said, 'You've got a helluva cheek, I must say. I don't have to concoct a plausible story, or any kind of story. My wife—' his voice shook a little— 'my wife committed suicide. I wasn't here when she did it, so I'm unable to explain the circumstances.'

'Surely you must have some idea why she would want to take her own life?'

'Oh, yes. She was very upset over the death of Mrs Davey. It depressed her more than I'd ever have imagined.'

'A young and healthy woman doesn't commit suicide just because a friend dies,' Piper said.

'In the case of an ordinary death, maybe not.' Heskett was trying to avoid looking at Julian Davey. 'But murder almost next-door isn't quite the same thing. My wife was inclined to be a bit highly-strung . . .'

'Even so, I doubt if it would've had that effect on her . . . unless, of course, she had her suspicions about you and Mrs Davey. Did she?'

'Every man his own psychiatrist,' Heskett said. He sounded just too off-hand.

Piper said, 'You can be as sarcastic as you like. It has been suggested that you returned home today in response to a phone call from your wife who told you she knew you'd been having an affair. That, however, wasn't everything.'

'Then—' Heskett played with the ends of his tie so as to

give his hands something to do—'then let's hear it all.'

'Very well. Your wife was out when Mrs Davey was murdered . . . so she couldn't know where you were or what you were doing at the time. We know, on your own admission, that you spent part of the afternoon in flat 2A. What we don't know is how long you were in the flat nor when you left. Neither did your wife . . . because it all happened during her absence. Do I make myself clear?'

Nothing stirred in Heskett's good-looking face. With the barest movement of his lips, he said, 'Go on.'

'It's reasonable to assume that she charged you with having been Mrs Davey's lover. So, if we take it a step further, the assumption must also be that your wife told you she believed you had killed Pauline Davey.'

Denial seemed too much effort for Neil Heskett. He said nothing.

Piper asked, 'Did you, Mr Heskett?'

In an explosive voice, Heskett said, 'No! No, I did not!'

Then the fit of violence drained out of him. He moistened his lips and added, 'Would I have admitted my relationship with her if I'd had anything to do with her death?'

'Quite possibly. You were forced into the admission.'

'You're crazy!'

Julian Davey had been listening in silence. Now he said, 'Everybody's crazy except you. But you're the beginning and end of the whole lousy business. If it hadn't been for you, none of this would've happened. Pauline and your own wife would still be alive.'

'Why should I have killed Pauline? Just tell me that. Why?'

'Maybe you didn't,' Piper said. 'But your wife thought you did. Either that was the reason she committed suicide or . . .'

'Well?'

'Or you got rid of her because she was about to betray you for the murder of Pauline Davey.'

'You're—' Heskett shook his head—'you're really serious, aren't you? You actually believe this cock-and-bull story.'

'Until you convince me otherwise,' Piper said.

'Commonsense should do that. How could I have made my wife do—' his voice was unsteady—'do what she did? You can't force a woman to gas herself.'

'It could've been done without force. Your best way of getting in the clear is to be completely frank about what took place between you and your wife at lunchtime today. Did she say it must've been you who murdered Pauline Davey?'

Davey felt the tip of his pointed nose while he watched Heskett intently. Piper wondered how long a wife could deceive her husband before his suspicions were aroused.

Indecision came and went in Heskett's eyes. Finally, he said, 'All right, I'll be frank with you. The answer is yes. She was in a state of hysterics when I arrived home and wouldn't let me get a word in edgeways. Called me every name under the sun. I tried to pacify her but it was no good. When I decided I'd better keep my mouth shut she took that as a confession of guilt. Next thing I knew she was saying I'd killed Pauline.'

'What did you do?'

'I told her she was stark raving mad. Then I walked out. What would you have done?'

Piper said, 'I prefer to think I'd never get into that kind of situation. However . . . Let's get back to Saturday afternoon. You were alone here in the flat?'

With barely-concealed relief, Heskett said, 'Yes. My wife went shopping when she'd washed-up after our midday meal.'

'What time did she go out?'

'About ten to three.'

'How did she think you were going to spend the afternoon?'

'I said I'd watch TV for an hour or so and maybe go to my club later if I got bored.'

'In actual fact, you visited Mrs Davey,' Piper said.

Heskett nodded. In Davey's face there was neither pain

nor anger. All emotion seemed to have drained out of him.

Without waiting to be asked, Heskett added, 'She'd told me to come in about half-past three.' He made it sound like a plain statement of fact.

'How did you get into flat 2A?'

'The two girls had given each other a spare key . . . in case one of them was out when a tradesman called.' He pointed to some keys on a hook alongside the kitchen door.

'What time did you leave her flat?'

'Nearly five o'clock . . .'

Somewhere in his mind Piper could hear a question and answer. Once again he remembered the wintry look in Superintendent Rillett's eyes.

'. . . *When does the doctor say death took place?*'

'*Within an hour prior to his examination. And he arrived at ten minutes to six . . .*'

Piper asked, 'Where was Mrs Davey when you left her?'

The knuckles of Davey's hands strained white as he listened. A muscle in his cheek had begun to twitch.

As though it meant nothing to him, Heskett said, 'She was in bed . . . asleep.'

'You're sure she was sleeping?'

'No, it isn't the kind of thing you can be sure of . . . but she looked asleep and I can't imagine why she'd want to pretend.'

'You went out without disturbing her?'

'Yes, of course.'

'Did you shut the outer door behind you?'

'Naturally.'

'Weren't you afraid of being seen when you left?'

In a matter-of-fact voice, Heskett said, 'I took care to avoid being seen.'

'If your wife had already returned home from her shopping expedition, I suppose you would have told her you'd been to your club?'

'That's right.'

'When did she return?'

'About a quarter of an hour later . . . say, five-fifteen.'

'After you came back to your own flat did you hear anyone going into or coming out of number 2A?'

Heskett took no time to think. He said, 'No, I never heard a thing until my wife came in.'

'If Mrs Davey had cried out would you have heard her?'

'I doubt it. I had the TV on . . . and the walls are pretty thick. Besides, the two flats aren't next-door to each other.'

Piper told himself all the parts of the story fitted. Perhaps they fitted too well.

As though Davey had the same thought, he said, 'You've only got one man's word for any of this. How do we know he isn't lying?'

'We don't. By the same token, what motive does he have to lie?'

'That's a good question,' Heskett said.

His voice and his face were just too smug. Piper said, 'I didn't mean you might not have a motive . . . just that I couldn't think of one. My only excuse is that I haven't had much experience of a man without any moral conscience—a man who can betray friend and wife and have no sense of guilt.'

An ugly colour darkened Heskett's good-looking face. He said, 'You mind your own damned business. I didn't ask for your opinion of my moral character.'

Julian Davey cleared his throat and said, 'You didn't ask for mine, either, but you're going to have it all the same. Piper's too gentle with you. My opinion is that you're a two-faced bastard. If I'd caught you with my wife on Saturday afternoon you wouldn't have been fit to go chasing women for many a long day.'

'But you didn't catch him,' Piper said. 'Funny when you come to think of it.'

With a wary look, Davey asked, 'What's so damn' funny?'

'The fact that you probably would have caught him if you'd come straight home from Queen's Park . . . assuming

Miss Ward is telling the truth when she says you left her at four-thirty.'

Davey's mouth opened and stayed open. He could find nothing to say.

Heskett began to laugh. He went on laughing although there was no amusement in his eyes.

At last he stopped and said, 'You're right, Mr Piper. It is funny when you come to think of it. Julian playing the outraged husband and, all the time, it was a case of what's sauce for the goose is sauce for the gander. Who is this Miss Ward?'

'An old friend of Mr Davey. According to her that's all she is—a friend from his pre-marriage days.'

'Do you believe that? If she was just a friend would he have lied to his wife? Would he have kidded her into thinking he was going to a football match? That kind of woman friend—'

'Shut up!' Davey said. His face was dark with anger. 'Don't you dare talk about her. No one with a mind like yours could understand a decent relationship. It's years since I last saw her. All we did was spend a couple of hours together chatting about old times. After what's happened I don't suppose I'll ever see her again.'

Piper said, 'If it was such an innocent meeting, why did you have to lie about it? You lied not only to me but also to the police. What do you think they're going to say when they hear where you really were on Saturday afternoon?'

'No one would ever have known if you—' Davey caught his breath—'if you hadn't interfered. There was nothing wrong in what happened. It made no difference to my wife that I wasn't at Highbury. She didn't care where I went . . . so long as I was out of the way.'

'Would you have told her?'

'That's none of your business. You've no right interrogating me like this in front of—' he gave Heskett a look of contempt—'in front of him.'

Neil Heskett said, 'I've heard of the pot calling the kettle black but this is ridiculous. He's been acting holier than thou and yet all the time he had a fancy woman of his own. How do you know he didn't get rid of Pauline so that he could marry this Miss Ward . . . or whatever she's called?'

'I don't,' Piper said.

In a strained voice, Davey asked, 'Whose side are you on? Aren't you supposed to be looking after my interests?'

'Not when you engaged me under false pretences. You can't expect loyalty from someone you don't trust. And you didn't give me your trust. All I got was a pack of lies.'

'Does that mean you're going to leave me flat?'

'No, it doesn't. What I do will depend on how honest you are with me. So I'll ask you again. If events hadn't turned out as they did, would you have told your wife you never went to the match at Highbury?'

It took Davey a long time to answer. He wrapped one hand alternately in the other, cleared his throat several times, glanced here and there as though seeking a way of escape.

At last, he said, 'I'm not sure.'

'Why not? Why shouldn't you have told her if your encounter—one single encounter—with Miss Ward was as innocent as you say?'

'Well, it's difficult to explain . . .'

'What's so difficult about it? Supposing I hadn't met you outside Denholme Court and you'd arrived home alone? If your wife had asked you how you'd enjoyed the match would you have said you hadn't gone to Highbury and admitted where you really had been all afternoon?'

'No, maybe not. You see—' Davey flapped his hands— 'the more I tried to explain the worse it would've sounded.'

'How could there have been anything wrong in a chance meeting with Miss Ward? Was your wife a jealous woman?'

'No, I wouldn't say that.'

'Then would you say she might not have believed you had met Miss Ward entirely by chance?'

'Oh, no. I hadn't any fear of that. It was just . . .' There he seemed to get lost in his thoughts.

'Just what?'

'She'd have—' he faltered and began again—'she'd have made me feel I'd been stupid . . . or, at least, rather indiscreet.'

'Well, you had been indiscreet, hadn't you?'

'I suppose so.'

His eyes flitted to Heskett and back to Piper and he asked, 'Do we have to go through all this while he's listening?'

'There's no harm in anyone hearing the truth,' Piper said. 'It can't hurt you.'

'If it is the truth,' Heskett said.

Julian Davey took a quick breath. He said, 'All right, Piper, so I was indiscreet. But I'd done nothing wrong. If things had worked out differently, it would've ended there.'

Piper said, 'What you're saying is that you had a slight feeling of guilt.'

'Yes . . . yes, I suppose so. Embarrassment would be a better word. I was reluctant to start something that would involve me in a lot of explanations.'

'Hence the answer you gave me when I asked you if you'd enjoyed the game.'

'Well, I wasn't obliged to tell you I hadn't gone. And since I anticipated that you'd meet my wife . . .' He lost himself again in the thought which followed.

It was feasible, Piper told himself. After the first lie, the rest had been inevitable. In the light of subsequent events, the deception had to be maintained.

His reason for that initial lie was easy to understand. He had not known his wife was dead—if he could be believed.

These awkward explanations which sounded so guilty could be indicative of his innocence. But perhaps that was Davey's intention. Perhaps he had planned right from the beginning to make a small admission conceal a greater guilt . . .

Piper asked, 'What time did you leave Miss Ward?'

The question seemed to come as a surprise. Davey was in no hurry to answer it.

When he could delay no longer, he said, 'As near as I recollect, it would be after half-past four.'

'How much after?'

'Five—ten minutes. What difference does it make?'

'Maybe a very big difference. If I know anything of the police they'll expect you to do a lot better than a blind guess. Among other things, they'll want to know why it took you a minimum of fifty minutes to do a journey which should've taken not much more than a quarter of an hour.'

Davey played with his hands again. Then he said, 'I stopped on the way home for a cup of coffee. Somewhere near Brondesbury Park station.'

'Why?'

'That's a damn' silly question! Do I have to explain that I was thirsty?'

'That's a damn' silly answer,' Piper said. 'You weren't so thirsty that you couldn't wait another fifteen or twenty minutes. Your real reason was, if I'm not mistaken, that you didn't want to get back before the time you would normally have returned home if you'd gone to Highbury. Isn't that so?'

In a reluctant voice, Davey said, 'Yes. I must admit I felt a certain amount of diffidence at the thought of having to explain . . .'

He looked at Heskett and then glanced quickly away and went on, 'I remember the name of the café if the police should want to know.'

Piper said, 'They certainly will . . . when I tell Superintendent Rillett what you should've told him long ago.'

CHAPTER XI

THE emergency staircase was semi-dark. One of the ceiling lamps had failed and the only light came from the turn in the landing.

As Piper began to go downstairs he heard footsteps on the floor above. They were not far behind him when he reached the ground floor, nearer still by the time he got to the entrance hall.

They gave him an uneasy feeling. He knew it was silly to be nervous but he had a strong compulsion to look back and see who was creeping up on him.

That thought in itself was even more absurd. There was nothing furtive about the footsteps now only a few paces behind him. Yet the feeling persisted . . .

Then a familiar voice said, 'Well, well, well! I thought I recognized that manly figure. What're you doing here?'

'I've just had a chat with Julian Davey and his neighbour in flat 2C,' Piper said.

'Have you now? Did you—' Quinn felt in his raincoat pockets and grunted with disappointment—'did you learn anything new?'

'Partly new, partly confirmation. You guessed right about Heskett. He admits he was Mrs Davey's lover. And I also got an admission from her husband. He wasn't at the football match on Saturday. He spent the afternoon with a woman he used to know before he got married.'

'Oh, indeed? When he says he knew her does he mean it in the Old Testament sense?'

'That's something we didn't dwell on,' Piper said. 'According to him they'd merely been friends. According to her she'd made a mistake in not marrying him. But I'll tell you all about it later. Where have you been?'

'Chatting with a very fetching lady in flat 3B on the top floor.' Quinn rummaged in the rest of his pockets and then asked, 'Would you happen to have a spare cigarette, by any chance?'

Piper said, 'Sorry, no. I've done what you should do—I've given up smoking. You'd feel a lot better if you did the same.'

With a sour look on his thin, pale face, Quinn said, 'You're all alike, you righteous abstainers. I ask for a cigarette—one lousy cigarette—and I get a moral lecture coupled with medical advice. Why don't you take your hat off and let everybody see your halo?'

'I'll overlook that,' Piper said. 'Who's the lady in flat 3B?'

'A Mrs Wrexham—widowed, attractive, old enough to know better, young enough to know how. If I'd known what she was like I'd have had a haircut before I went calling on her.'

'What did she have to say?'

'Not very much—but interesting. Seems that Sergeant Langdon has interviewed her and she's told me what she told him. She was at the Armada Casino on Friday night and heard that the late Pauline Davey had won a packet.'

'Where did she hear it?'

'From Mrs Davey herself, no less. In the course of their conversation, the same Mrs Davey also let fall that she hadn't much time for her husband. To this, Mrs Wrexham now adds that she's had her suspicions for some time about Pauline and the good-looking bloke in No. 2C—to wit, Neil Heskett.'

'Doesn't add anything to what we already had,' Piper said.

The sour look returned to Quinn's face. He said, 'I've got an idea I'm flogging a dead horse. How was I supposed to know you'd squeezed the truth out of Heskett?'

'You weren't. And there is one thing. Would you say we can rely on what Mrs Wrexham says about Pauline Davey—that she hadn't much time for her husband?'

'Sounded in good faith to me,' Quinn said. 'In the light of everything we now know about Pauline and lover-boy, I'm not surprised her husband played second fiddle. I'd say he was lucky to be in the band at all.'

That fleeting picture of a man outside the sitting-room door with a tray passed through Piper's mind. It had a meaning he still failed to grasp—a meaning reinforced by the piece of gossip that Quinn had picked up from Mrs Wrexham.

If the Daveys had been on strained terms . . . if Julian had suspected that his wife was unfaithful . . . if that encounter at the casino between Davey and Susan Ward had not been their first meeting . . . His activity in the kitchen might well have represented nothing more than an act for Piper's benefit.

Davey had known an insurance man would be visiting the flat at half-past five. Davey could have made his arrangements in advance so that there would be a witness present.

Yet . . . The police would check with the café where he said he had gone after he left Susan Ward. And Davey knew that. So he must be able to account for the whole of the time between four-thirty and five-thirty.

Even if he had not been with Miss Ward until half-past four, it still made no difference. Pauline was alive when Heskett left the flat. And that was nearly five o'clock. If Heskett had told the truth . . . if . . . if . . .

Quinn said, 'I don't know where you are but I'm still here. Do you often go into a trance?'

'I was trying to work out how Davey could've done it,' Piper said.

'What you mean is that he couldn't.'

'Not unless the police surgeon has got the time of death wrong.'

'It's possible . . . but unlikely.'

'I'd say it can be ruled out.'

'Then we have to look elsewhere,' Quinn said. 'I was thinking I'd have a word with Mrs Wilson in 1A. She's lived here a long time and she's bound to know all about everybody's affairs. Care to join me?'

'I can't see any reason why I shouldn't.' Piper said.

There was an inspection lens at head-height in the door.

Quinn brought his face close to it after he had rung the bell.

He said, 'Watch the birdie . . .'

There were shuffling footsteps, the rattle of keys, heavy breathing as someone inside struggled to draw back a bolt that needed oiling. When the door at last opened it was held by the length of a safety chain. Through the gap they could see the face of an old woman.

She was tall and angular and stooped with age. Her sallow face sagged, her small bright eyes were like the hooded eyes of a lizard. In their depths Quinn saw the alert intelligence of a mind much younger than her body.

When she had studied him critically she turned her attention to Piper, her pallid lips tightly compressed, one bony hand clinging to the edge of the door. She had the air of aloofness which belongs to the elderly.

Quinn said, 'Good evening. Mrs Wilson?'

'Yes. Who are you?' Her voice was thin but clear and precise.

'I'm from the *Morning Post*. The name's Quinn. This is Mr Piper, a colleague of mine.'

'Oh, yes. What do you want?'

'We'd like to talk to you about what's been happening upstairs.'

She gave him a dry, wrinkled smile which made him feel there was a gap of many generations between them. She said, 'You mean you want me to talk to you . . . isn't that it?'

'Well, if you wish to put it that way—yes.'

'It's the correct way to put it. I believe that people should say what they mean and mean what they say.'

Her eyes flitted to Piper's face. She asked, 'Why should I talk about that tiresome young woman who went seeking trouble and found it?'

'Because you may be able to help,' Piper said.

'Bit late to help her. And, as for her husband, I've never any sympathy for a man who lets his wife make a fool of him. Besides, you shouldn't need me. You were there when she was found.'

Quinn coughed and said, 'You're certainly well informed.'

The look in Mrs Wilson's eyes reminded him of his schooldays. She said, 'That's why you're here, isn't it? You've been told I know everybody else's business.'

'That's right,' Quinn said.

'Ah, now—' she gave him another smile that had no more warmth than the first one—'now we're beginning to understand each other. Say what you mean and mean what you say—that's my motto.'

Piper asked, 'Then may we come in?'

'Of course. I like a bit of company. But you'll have to wait until I get this chain off. I've as many bolts and bars and locks as the Bastille. It'd be God help me if there was a fire. My son always thinks somebody's going to break in and carry me off . . .'

She was complaining to herself while she closed the door, unfastened the chain and opened the door again. On halting feet she led them into a sitting-room furnished with solid old chairs, a high-backed settee, a carved dining-table, a sideboard that filled almost the whole length of one wall.

There were antique ornaments, faded loose rugs and a big mirror with a heavy gilt frame. The whole place looked like a repository for second-hand furniture.

Mrs Wilson positioned herself under the low-power ceiling light, her arms folded. She said, 'I haven't had so many visitors in months. First that detective-superintendent and after him a sergeant . . . now you two. If I were any younger I'd be flattered. But it isn't my company you want . . . and I can't tell you any more than I told the police. They didn't find me much help.'

'We don't expect a lot,' Piper said.

'In that case you won't be disappointed. I never saw any strangers coming in or out all Saturday afternoon—except you, of course—and I didn't hear anything.'

'Where were you when you saw me?'

'At the window. I was there for most of three hours. It's

where I spend many an afternoon. Not much else to do at my time of life. On Sundays the family take me out. Saturdays I'm generally on my own. Didn't speak to a soul all day except Sherwood. He's the caretaker.'

'I've met him,' Quinn said.

'Yes, he told me you'd been asking him questions. He was scared you might mention his name when you talked to Mr Heskett. Not that it isn't true. I've had my own ideas for a long time about Heskett and Pauline Davey.'

'You didn't see Mr Davey go out?'

'No . . . but Sherwood told me he'd seen him drive out of the garage about half-past one.'

'What time did Mrs Heskett go out?'

'Not long before three. About ten minutes to the hour, as near as I remember.'

With the same hard bright look in her eyes, Mrs Wilson went on, 'Silly woman . . . such a silly woman. I'd have thought she had more sense than to go and put her head in the gas oven. Oh, I know she must've guessed her husband had been carrying-on with Mrs Davey but no man's worth it. I say that although I was happily married for over forty years . . .'

She was going on when Piper asked, 'Did you see Mrs Heskett come back?'

'Yes. That would be near enough a quarter past five. Sherwood saw her, too. He was in here fixing one of the window catches. I didn't say anything to him but I thought to myself she'd been out since before three and Mr Davey left at half-past one . . . and there's an old saying that when the cat's away the mice will play.'

'What did you think when you heard that Mrs Davey had been murdered?'

'To tell you the truth—' there was not even a trace of compassion in Mrs Wilson's old lined face—'I wondered if her husband had found out she'd been making a fool of him. Of course, that was before I got to know she was dead when he returned home.'

All Piper's random impressions coalesced into one central

core. Time after time he had come to the same impasse: she was dead when Davey returned home. It was like a recurring refrain in his head.

Quinn said, 'Flat 2A is immediately above here, isn't it?'

Mrs Wilson looked at him, her mouth old and dry and puckered. She said, 'Yes . . . but I can only say to you what I kept saying to the police. These flats are pretty solidly built. They'd have to be making a lot of noise in any one of them before I'd hear a thing. How do you know, anyway, that Mrs Davey got the chance to call for help?'

'We don't,' Quinn said. 'Only one person knows whether she did or not. And if that person got in through the rear door from the gardens at the back . . .'

'I doubt if we'll ever know,' Mrs Wilson said.

Piper could hear noises in a room not far away . . . footsteps . . . a brief spell of knocking . . . someone whistling quietly. Once again he remembered the radio he had imagined was playing in Mrs Pauline Davey's bedroom.

There had been that thread of music and farther off a murmur of voices. He had never located the source of those voices . . . but the music had not come from Mrs Davey's room. It was still playing when he walked in and found Davey staring down at his wife's pale dead face.

If a distant radio could be heard and far-off voices came through as well, Mrs Wilson must be dull of hearing. That should hardly be a cause for surprise. She seemed to have all her other faculties . . . and some impairment to one of them was only to be expected at her age.

He said, 'Forgive my asking, Mrs Wilson, but is there somebody else in the flat?'

She unfolded her arms and put her hands behind her back and smiled the withered smile which meant nothing. She said, 'You don't need to apologize. I'm past the time of life when I can be compromised. What you hear is the caretaker. I wouldn't let him finish the odds and ends on Sunday out of respect for my neighbours and so he came in again tonight.'

The shadow of loneliness momentarily dimmed her small

sharp eyes as she added, 'If you hadn't called on me, at least it would've been someone to talk to.'

There was an integrity, an air of directness, about her that appealed to Piper. Yet in some ways she was a strange old woman. Perhaps he knew too little about old women to understand them. Perhaps Mrs Wilson was different from the others.

Another thought grew out of nowhere. Perhaps she had learned the trick of being able to hide anything she had no wish to reveal. Perhaps she could tell him what had happened at Denholme Court on Saturday afternoon . . .

It was a thought without substance. This elderly woman no longer took an active part in the lives of others. As the years advanced she had withdrawn from life. She knew only what she was told, only what she saw from her sitting-room window.

Age had dried up the sap in her emotions as well as her body. She seemed detached from sympathy, to feel no pity for the two young women who had died before they had lived half their days.

People talked about the selfishness of the old. Perhaps age had taught Mrs Wilson that she had to think of herself, that no one else cared about her likes and dislikes. Now the years had built a protective shell around her. Maybe it kept out thoughts of the darkness to come . . .

He wondered what change would take place in his personality if he lived to see old age. By that time many of his contemporaries would be dead. Each year he would become more and more alone . . . like Mrs Wilson.

As he rid himself of his morbid vision of the future that might never be there was a light tap at the door. It opened a few inches and a man's voice said, 'I've finished, Mrs Wilson. Would you like to take a look before I go?'

Now Piper could see him—a tallish man balding at the front. He had the weatherbeaten look of someone who spent a lot of time out-of-doors.

When he caught sight of Quinn and Piper, he said, 'Oh, sorry if I've interrupted. Didn't know you had company.'

Mrs Wilson said, 'They won't mind. Have you done the kitchen cupboard?'

'Yes, it's OK now. You shouldn't have any more trouble.'

'I'll be sending for you if I have. Come in and see me in the morning and I'll settle up.'

'That's all right,' Sherwood said. 'No hurry. Good night, Mrs Wilson.'

He glanced at Quinn, gave Piper a short nod, and added, 'Good night, gentlemen . . .'

After he had gone, Mrs Wilson stood placidly waiting, her sharp little eyes on Piper's face. At last, she said, 'You remind me of my late husband. He was an understanding man, a man who could see beyond the outward appearances. You think before you speak. He was like that, too.'

'Thank you for the compliment,' Piper said.

'It wasn't meant as a compliment. With some people I can say what I feel. It's a kind of instinct. I wish you could stay for a while . . . but I suppose you have places to go.'

'I'm afraid so. My wife will be expecting me home soon. I left a note telling her I wouldn't be late.'

'Very well. Perhaps some other time if you're passing this way . . .'

'I'll call in and say hallo,' Piper said.

With no sarcasm in her voice, she said, 'That'll be nice to think about . . . even if you never do. Anticipation is half the pleasure in life.'

Quinn shuffled his feet and coughed. He said, 'I must be going as well. Before I leave would you mind if I asked you one more question?'

'No.' She looked at him as though from a long way off. 'If I'd had any objections I wouldn't have let you in. But I still say all the questions in the world won't get you anywhere.'

'I'd like your answer, nevertheless. On Saturday afternoon were you sitting at the window for the whole of those three hours?'

Mrs Wilson said, 'The police asked me that and I told them there were only two occasions when I left the window.

One was to let Sherwood in. That would be a minute or so after half-past two. He rang the bell just as I was making myself comfortable.'

'And the second time?'

'I went to brew him a pot of tea about a quarter to five.'

'How long did that take?'

'A couple of minutes. My electric kettle is very quick.'

'So you must've been back at the window before ten to five?'

'Yes, I was.' She sounded irritable.

'And you didn't see Mr Davey at any time after that until he returned at five-thirty?'

'No, I didn't. You're as bad as the police. The answers you'd like are those that fit your own ideas. Well, I'm not going to let anybody put words in my mouth.'

'I wouldn't—' Quinn followed Piper to the door—'I wouldn't dream of trying.'

They were going out when Mrs Wilson said, 'If Mr Davey had come back at any time before half-past five, I'd know who killed his wife . . . and so would you.'

CHAPTER XII

THE moon had climbed up into a sky filled with stars by the time they got to Fleet Street. In the past hour and a half it had become much colder.

As Quinn got out of the car, he asked, 'You going straight home?'

Piper said, 'No, I'll give Rillett a call first. He may still be in his office and I'd like him to know what transpired at my meeting with Davey and Heskett. It's the sort of thing he ought to be told right away.'

'Yes, I suppose so. If I'm any judge of the superintendent, Pauline Davey's boy-friend is going to find life somewhat trying when the police learn he was the last person to see her alive.'

'Not quite the last. There was the person who stabbed her to death with the pair of scissors.'

'Might be one and the same,' Quinn said. 'Wouldn't be the first time a married man got tired of his unwanted mistress. Night-night . . . and thanks for the ride. May give you a ring tomorrow.'

The switchboard said Superintendent Rillett had not yet gone home. '. . . If you hold the line I'll see if he's available.'

While Piper waited he thought of Jane. She would be wondering what had happened to him.

. . . Fortunately she won't worry. Never been the worrying type. In that respect she's like Ann. And in other respects, too. I'm a lucky man. Maybe I don't fully appreciate just how lucky . . .

Out of his subconscious came a thought that had never occurred to him before. Jane meant the whole world to him. Supposing he had met her while Ann was alive . . .

Other men had loved two women at the same time. He

had been speaking to a man like that within the past couple of hours. In Heskett's case it might be suggested that love was no part of his relationship with Pauline Davey, that she merely satisfied an animal appetite. But only Neil Heskett knew how they had really felt about each other.

... What would have happened if I had met Jane before Ann was killed in the accident? No one could've supplanted Ann. Yet they would've been so much alike ...

There he recognized the fallacy. Jane was not Jane while Ann was alive. He would not have been able to see Jane as he saw her now. He would have had no need of her. That was where he differed from men like Heskett.

Once more there was the sound of music in his head, once more he was listening to a man's voice in an adjoining room. His mind supplied four haunting words of the lyric.

'... *You forgot to remember* ...'

He should feel no guilt because he had re-married. Ann would not have wanted him to spend the rest of his days in loneliness. She herself would have chosen Jane to share his empty life.

No man was intended to live alone. Jane was right for him. Jane was Ann all over again. Through her he had been able to build something strong out of the broken remnants of the past.

And behind his new existence there lay a gentle memory of long ago. He had not forgotten. That memory would never harm what he and Jane had created together ... but he would always remember the once-upon-a-time.

He had kept faith far beyond the bounds of fidelity. That was where he was different from a man like Neil Heskett.

Then the phone said, 'Good evening, Mr Piper. Must be important if you're ringing me at this hour.'

'I've come across some information that I felt you ought to know as soon as possible,' Piper said. 'Among other things, Julian Davey didn't go to the match at Highbury on Saturday afternoon.'

'Indeed? And where did he go?'

'To the Armada Casino where he met—apparently by

chance—someone he used to know. He spent a couple of hours in her company and, when he left her about half-past four, stopped for a cup of coffee on his way home with the idea of filling in time so that he wouldn't arrive back at Denholme Court before five-thirty.'

The superintendent said, 'Interesting . . . very interesting. How do you know all this?'

Piper told him. When Rillett had heard it all he asked no questions and he had only one comment to make.

'. . . If it's true that Mrs Heskett believed her husband killed Pauline Davey then that lets Davey out so far as Mrs Heskett is concerned. He had no motive for wanting to get rid of her.'

'Only if Heskett's telling the truth,' Piper said.

'That goes without saying. But I'm inclined to think he is. A man doesn't usually lie when it means he's directing suspicion at himself. That's all he has achieved. His own story leaves him without a shred of an alibi for the time when Mrs Davey was murdered.'

'And he didn't only admit the whole thing to me. Julian Davey was present as well.'

'Which makes me feel that Heskett may have been an unfaithful husband and a false friend—but he didn't kill his mistress. If he had you'd have got nothing out of him.'

'Seems logical enough. The question is what you can do now.'

'I'll get him to make a signed statement,' Rillett said. 'That'll do for a start. Then he can't refuse to let me search his flat for any garments with bloodstains on them.'

'What about Davey?'

'He's going to explain where he was every minute of the time last Saturday afternoon and what sort of relationship he has with this woman Susan Ward. Then I'll want to know his reason for saying he'd been to a football match at Highbury. He'll find I'm harder to convince than you are. In my book a man doesn't deceive his wife—or intend to deceive her—unless he has something to hide.'

'Nevertheless, you'll admit it's quite a plausible explanation,' Piper said.

'Maybe just too plausible. Julian Davey has an answer for everything. When I find that one of them was a deliberate lie I'm entitled to doubt all the others . . . and I do. You know where that leaves him, don't you?'

The picture of a man outside the sitting-room door flitted through Piper's mind again. Its impression still lingered as he said, 'Heskett says Mrs Davey was alive when he left the flat at approximately five o'clock. If you verify that Davey was in a coffee shop near Brondesbury Park station until after five, then he couldn't have done it. There wasn't enough time.'

In a grumbling voice, Rillett said, 'Don't quote me . . . but I'll bet a week's wages Mister Julian Davey's alibi comes up smelling of sweet violets. That's what makes me distrust everything about him. He's just too, too innocent.'

'Does that automatically make him guilty?'

'No, of course not! If you weren't looking after his interests you'd know what I mean.'

'I do know what you mean. I'm not leaning over backwards to protect him. If I discover he's been telling me other lies I'll drop him like a hot brick.'

There was a measure of conflict in Piper's mind. He had kept one thing back—one thing which might have a bearing on the events of Saturday afternoon. Yet to reveal it meant breaking his word to Susan Ward.

He could hear himself saying '. . . *Providing he's innocent, I won't betray your trust.*'

And she had trusted him. She had admitted there had been more in her former association with Julian Davey than ordinary friendship.

Piper remembered the exact phrase she had used. '. . . *If I hadn't taken so long to make up my mind I'd have married Julian . . . and perhaps none of this would've happened . . .*'

It might not be relevant. It might not add anything to the view that Rillett already held. And, when all was said and done, Davey's innocence or guilt depended on where he had been between a few minutes to five and a few minutes past five that afternoon.

Superintendent Rillett said, 'One lie is enough for me. Now that he's admitted he wasn't at the match, who's to say where he was all afternoon? Why should I believe what this woman Ward told you?'

'Whether you believe her or not is immaterial,' Piper said. 'All you have to do is prove that Davey either never went to the coffee shop at all or that he left in time to arrive home shortly after five o'clock. If you can't—'

'I'll have to look elsewhere,' Rillett said.

'Afraid so. Heskett would be the obvious choice except that he was too honest about Pauline Davey and his wife's allegations. If he were your man he'd have to be mad to admit all that in front of two witnesses.'

The phone went quiet. While Piper waited he could hear someone tapping rhythmically at the other end of the line.

Then Superintendent Rillett said, 'You and I have had a long day. I'm going to let you go home to your wife. If you should think of anything . . .'

'I'll let you know.'

'Thanks. This looks like being a tough one to crack. Too many people could've wanted to see Mrs Pauline Davey dead. And only her friendly neighbour, Mrs Heskett, isn't in a position to deny it.'

'You think she might've found out what her husband was up to?'

'Yes. So does Quinn, crime reporter extraordinary . . . and I mean extraordinary.'

Piper said, 'If it was Mrs Heskett, how did she get into flat 2A? I know she and her neighbour exchanged spare keys but the one for 2A was used by Neil Heskett on Saturday afternoon . . . so it couldn't have been in his wife's possession when she went out at ten to three . . . could it?'

'Don't ask me. Every way I turn I come up against how this and how that.'

In his gentle patient voice, Rillett added, 'There's an old adage that tomorrow's another day. At this time of night it's quite a comfort. All the questions that plague me will still be here in the morning . . . but I'll have had a few hours to recuperate . . .'

His voice became fainter. '. . . Good night, Mr Piper. Thank you for your co-operation. I can use plenty of it.'

Once or twice next morning, and again later in the day, Piper had that mental picture of a man with a laden tea-tray. He could see it more clearly now, he could hear the rattle of dishes as Davey juggled with the tray while he opened his wife's bedroom door.

But the recollection still had no meaning, still conveyed nothing more to him than a feeling of frustration. It should mean something—something belonging to his memory of that moment when he entered the bedroom and saw Julian Davey staring down at his wife's dead face. But the clue lay just beyond Piper's reach.

Quinn phoned on Tuesday. He rang again on Wednesday to discuss the same things they had talked about the day before. All their talk solved nothing.

Lunchtime on Thursday Piper found himself thinking about a man called Davey—a man who had promised to take his wife a cup of tea when he returned from the football match at Highbury. This time the picture in Piper's mind was more vivid than ever. He saw the tray with a cup and saucer . . . a tea pot . . . a sugar bowl . . .

Then he had the answer. Then he saw what he should have seen right from the beginning.

Realization was an almost frightening thing. So simple . . . and yet so terrible. Now he knew he had stumbled on what might well be the secret of Pauline Davey's death.

CHAPTER XIII

QUINN thought it was possible. '... With respect, Mr Piper, sir, you've got a nasty mind. I could never have imagined anything like that. It's beyond my conception . . . as her ladyship said when she was asked if she bred her own poodles. The question is what you're going to do about it.'

'What can I do? There isn't a scrap of proof.'

'And no hope of any. People would say you've let your imagination run away with you.'

'That's why you're the only one I've told so far.'

'Well, now you've got my reaction, how about seeing what Solemn Sammy thinks?'

'Not yet,' Piper said. 'I'd like to take it a stage further myself.'

'How?'

'By trying it out on Julian Davey.'

'Now that would be something,' Quinn said. 'When do you propose doing it?'

'Have to be when he's on his own. I'll make an appointment to see him at Denholme Court tonight.'

'Mind if I come along?'

'I'd be glad of your support,' Piper said.

Seconds after he had hung up, his phone rang. He thought Quinn had forgotten something. The amount of time that man wasted . . .

It was Julian Davey. He said, 'I've been thinking over what happened the other night in Heskett's flat.'

'And?'

'Well, it seems obvious to me you don't believe a word I say. You went and questioned Miss Ward as if you were trying to catch me out and then on Monday night—'

'Why should I believe you? That business about where you were Saturday afternoon was fundamental and yet you let me go on thinking you were at the match. How do you expect me to help you?'

'I explained why I did that . . . and I hoped you'd understand. All the rest was true.'

'How do I know? How can I be sure of anything?'

Davey said, 'All right, if that's the way you feel, drop the whole thing. Send me your bill and I'll let you have a cheque by return.'

'There's no hurry. Before you dispense with my services I want to ask you a very special question.'

'Ask me whatever you like. I've got nothing to hide.'

'This can't be discussed over the phone,' Piper said. 'Will you be at home all evening?'

'No, I'm going away shortly for a long week-end. After what's been happening I can't stand the sight of my flat. I must have a break . . . even if it's only a few days.'

'When are you leaving?'

'In about an hour. My car's being serviced and, soon as it's ready, I'll be off. Haven't even booked anywhere. It'll be a case of stopping when the mood takes me.'

'We should have a chat before you go,' Piper said.

'Won't it keep until Tuesday? I'll be back by then and we can meet here or at your office or wherever you wish.'

'It won't keep. In all fairness—' the music of that old song was tinkling again inside Piper's head—'I must talk to you in private now.'

Davey said, 'If it's so very important, I'll pop in when I've collected my car. I'm in no particular rush. See you between half-past three and four o'clock . . .'

A man in Editorial said Quinn had gone out. '. . . No idea where but he told me he'd be back before six. Can I give him a message?'

'Ask him to phone me when he gets in,' Piper said.

He felt increasingly on edge as the next half-hour went by. If he were right it no longer mattered where Julian Davey had been on Saturday afternoon. His wife was alive at, or near, five o'clock . . . so the time factor could be ignored.

... *If I'm right. Can't do any harm even if I'm wrong. Won't be the first crazy idea I've had. Davey's going to be annoyed but it won't worry me if I rub him the wrong way. After the way he's behaved I don't care how much I annoy him. He's asked for it ... even if I'm wrong ...*

There were several things Piper had to deal with but he found it difficult to concentrate. His eyes kept straying to the desk clock and he lost the thread of what he was doing. Eventually he put his papers away. Forcing himself would do no good.

So he sat and watched the clock. Three-thirty became four ... and four became four-fifteen. There was still no sign of Julian Davey at half-past four.

All his office numbers were engaged. Piper tried twice. He was about to try once again when Davey arrived.

His florid face was irritable and he looked like a man on the verge of losing his temper. He said, 'I won't apologize for being late because it's really your fault. If you hadn't gone poking and prying I wouldn't have been subjected to all this carry-on.'

'What carry-on?'

'Superintendent Rillett called on me just as I was leaving to come here. Acted so damn' superior you'd have thought I was a criminal.'

Piper said, 'Well, you haven't been exactly helpful, have you, considering he's investigating the murder of your wife? By lying, you provided the police with a stick to beat you. At best it was stupid. No wonder you were scared they'd get their claws into you.'

'All right, so I was scared.' Davey pulled at his pointed nose as though it itched. 'That's why I engaged you. And a helluva lot of good you've been. Thanks to you, my situation is worse instead of better.'

'Blame yourself for that. A man who tells lies to the police is just asking for trouble.'

'I've explained that over and over again. There wouldn't have been any trouble if you'd been acting for me and not against me.'

'Acting for you didn't mean concealing evidence,' Piper said.

'You talk just like—' Davey flapped his hands in exasperation—'just like Superintendent Rillett. Hauled me over the coals for saying I'd gone to Highbury. He's already questioned Miss Ward and he warned me I'd be in real hot water if I didn't stick to the truth from now on.'

In a surly voice, Davey added, 'The annoying thing is that this is all your work.'

'On Monday night I told you I had no choice but to inform the police. From the very start I made it clear I wouldn't cover up for you.'

'I never asked you to cover up anything. Even Rillett admits it doesn't matter whether I was at the match or not.'

'Has he verified that you went to a coffee shop near Brondesbury Park station after you left Miss Ward?'

'Yes, of course. The girl behind the counter remembered me because she thought I looked like a politician she'd seen on TV.'

'Did she also remember how long you were in the coffee shop?'

'Fortunately, yes. She assured Rillett I was there until after five o'clock.'

Piper had known what the answer would be. It made no real difference. The time factor was now irrelevant.

He said, 'Very fortunate.'

A look of suspicion came into Davey's eyes. He asked, 'What's that supposed to mean?'

'Only that the superintendent is quite right. It doesn't matter what you did between half-past one and five o'clock Saturday afternoon. The vital thing could have been where you were just after five.'

'Well, it isn't vital any more. Rillett knows exactly where I was. And I'm up to—' he put a hand to his throat—'up to here with all these insinuations that I had anything to do with what happened to my wife. I loved her and trusted her and—'

'And she betrayed you,' Piper said. 'There's only your word that you didn't know she was Heskett's mistress. If it could be proved you did know . . .'

With cold precision, Davey said, 'I didn't. I never dreamed there was anything between them. Get that into your head, once and for all. I've told Rillett I won't stand for any more of his persecution . . . and that goes for you, too. If you're so keen on finding out who killed my wife, why don't you try to squeeze the truth out of Neil Heskett?'

'He had no motive,' Piper said.

'Don't be so sure of that just because you can't think of one. The important thing to me is that he's got no alibi, either.'

'But you have,' Piper said. 'When we clear away all the lies and the deception we find you're able to account for every minute of your time from one-thirty until after five o'clock. In other words, telling lies showed a dividend. It focused attention on your visit to the Armada Casino, your innocent get-together with Miss Ward, your call at the coffee shop. Fits very neatly, doesn't it?'

'I don't—' Julian Davey looked and sounded bewildered —'I just don't know what you're talking about. If I must treat it seriously, tell me why I had to go to the casino and involve Susan Ward. The superintendent was only interested in where I was around five o'clock. Since my wife was killed shortly after five—'

'That's only an assumption,' Piper said. 'It's possible— just possible—that she was still alive at five-thirty.'

Davey took a long slow breath. He said, 'I give up. It was as near as dammit half-past five when we went upstairs. We didn't see anybody leaving the flat and no one left after we went in. You're not saying that the person who killed her vanished in a puff of smoke, are you?'

'No. I've got an idea, for what it's worth, that there were only three people in the flat: you and I . . . and your wife. She was asleep in the bedroom.'

'How could she—' Davey choked over the next word and

began again—'how could she have been asleep when I found her dead only a few minutes later? Do you know what you're saying?'

'Oh, yes. Of course, I admit it's only an idea but I wanted to see what you thought before I mentioned it to Superintendent Rillett. In fairness to you—'

'Don't be so damned hypocritical! What is this absurd idea you've got?'

'It isn't absurd,' Piper said. 'It's quite simple. When you went into your wife's bedroom you could've had that pair of scissors on the tea-tray.'

Julian Davey's mouth opened and he stood for a long moment with a stupid look on his face. He seemed to have lost the power of speech.

While he was trying to find the right words, Piper added, 'Only an idea, as I say. But you could have put the tray down on the other bed, drawn back your wife's bedclothes and covered her mouth with your free hand. Wakened suddenly and hardly able to breathe, she wouldn't have made a sound while you stabbed her to death.'

As though it took a great effort, Davey swallowed, sucked in a breath and swallowed again. In a dry voice, he said, 'I've never heard anything so outrageous in all my life. You really believe I could do a thing like that while you were next door in the sitting-room . . .'

His throat cleared. He was shaking with fury as he went on, 'Send me your bill but don't dare come near me if you know what's good for you! I never want to see you again! Do you understand? Keep away from me! That's all . . . just keep away from me.'

He stopped shaking and his face became very pale. Without looking back he went out and slammed the office door behind him.

Piper told himself nothing had been settled either way. Whatever he had hoped to achieve, the results were negative. He could think what he liked but he still had no proof.

Superintendent Rillett was unlikely to do any better. He would have to know what had happened and he might say

Davey had now been put on his guard. It made no difference what he said. He would have to be told . . .

Just before six o'clock the phone rang. As he picked up the receiver, Piper wondered what effect Quinn would have had on Davey. Two might have succeeded where one had failed. Unfortunate that Quinn had had to go out.

It was not Quinn. A woman's thin voice said, 'Mr Piper? This is Mrs Wilson. You called on me at Denholme Court the other night . . . remember?'

Piper said, 'Yes, of course. What can I do for you, Mrs Wilson?'

'Well, I've been thinking over that business we talked about when you were here with that man Quinn.'

'Yes?'

'In my opinion you're all rushing round and getting nowhere. That goes for the police, too. Not that I'm trying to be clever . . . but when you've lived to my age you can see further than most and I think everybody's looking at it the wrong way.'

'What do you mean by that?'

'It was two of them. That's what I mean. As I was saying to Mrs Wrexham this morning—'

Her voice broke off and Piper could hear a bell ringing in the background. Then Mrs Wilson said, 'It's my butcher with the week-end joint. I'll have to go and pay him. If you're interested in the idea I've got come and see me.'

'When?'

'Any time. Soon as you like. I'm not going anywhere. I've had my evening meal so you can suit yourself. But I don't think you'll find it's a wasted journey.'

Piper said, 'All right, Mrs Wilson. I'll be with you as soon after six as I can make it.'

CHAPTER XIV

QUINN PHONED at five past six. He said, 'I was out covering a police manhunt for that fellow they want to question about the shooting of a copper in Blackpool. Just got back. Have you fixed up a date with Julian Davey?'

'No. I've already spoken to him . . . but I'll tell you about that later. As it happens, I'm going out to Denholme Court because Mrs Wilson would like to see me. She rang ten minutes ago.'

'What does she want?'

'Got some idea concerning the murder of Mrs Davey. Thinks we're all on the wrong track. Fancy coming along?'

'Sure. That old faggot has all her wits about her. If she says she's got an idea it's bound to be a good one. When are you going?'

'As soon as you can get here. Better take a taxi and pick me up at the corner of Vigo Street.'

'Taxi, eh? There's posh for you . . . as the parson said when they told him the bride wasn't pregnant.'

'If you waste time with a lot of nonsense I'll go without you.'

'Don't hector me,' Quinn said. 'I'm on my way . . .'

He had difficulty finding a taxi and traffic caused further delay. It was almost half-past six when he reached Vigo Street. By then it had begun to rain.

Traffic congestion made them lose more time on their way out to Hampstead. They arrived at Cornstalk Avenue not much before seven o'clock.

Piper thought it was a shame to keep the old lady waiting so long. '. . . She'll think I'm not coming.'

'The longer she waits the greater the pleasure she'll get from anticipation,' Quinn said.

When they got to Denholme Court it was raining heavily.

He tumbled out of the taxi and sprinted to the entrance, his lank hair flopping in his eyes. Piper was only a couple of paces behind him.

The entrance hall lights were on. In flat 1B Piper could hear a rumbling voice followed by a burst of laughter and applause. Then a second voice began talking rapidly.

Quinn said, 'Isn't the telly marvellous? Millions of people seated before their household altar, all worshipping the same gods at the same time, all hypnotized into a state where they'll believe that so-and-so washes whiter or tastes better or lasts longer or sells cheaper or makes you smell nicer or look sexier or grow thinner or keep warmer or grow richer . . . ad infinitum, ad nauseam.'

'Ad nauseam is right,' Piper said. 'I'm not interested in TV advertising. All I want is to hear what Mrs Wilson has to say and then I'll get off home.'

He touched the bell-push, listened for a few moments and touched it again. There was no reply. As he was about to try once more, the phone began ringing.

It rang only three or four times. When it stopped, Quinn said, 'If it's a chatty friend of the old woman who's on the line, you'll be late getting home. Give the door bell another go.'

Piper was unable to hear anybody talking on the phone and yet he got no answer when he rang the bell again and again. He said, 'I know she's a bit deaf but she should've heard me by now. The bell makes enough noise.'

'Not when you're a hundred years old and you've got your ear glued to the phone,' Quinn said.

'But she isn't talking.'

'Maybe that's because she can't get a word in edgeways. With some people all you do is listen.'

'I know exactly what you mean,' Piper said.

'Har-har . . . funny man. You can do what you like but I'm not hanging around here all night. I think I'll take a look through the sitting-room window. The light was on. I saw it as we were coming in . . .'

He went along the hall and out through the swing doors.

As he disappeared from sight, Piper discovered that the door of flat 1A was not properly locked. The last time it had been shut, the latch had failed to engage. When he gave the door a little push it opened enough to show him that Mrs Wilson had not secured it with the safety-chain.

An old woman living alone should have learned to be more careful. He remembered her saying '. . . It'd be God help me if there was a fire. My son always thinks somebody's going to break in and carry me off.'

She might not be the nervous type but prudence cost nothing and there was no sense in taking unnecessary risks. After what had happened so recently to people on the floor above, a woman of her age . . .

He pushed the door wider open. When he could still hear nothing, he called out, 'Mrs Wilson? Are you there?'

That was when Quinn came back. He said, 'You can see through a chink in the net curtains . . . and she's not using the phone.'

As he came closer he saw the open door. With a strange look on his thin pale face, he asked, 'How did you manage that?'

'It wasn't properly locked,' Piper said. 'I happened to press against it and the latch yielded.'

'Queer . . . You'd almost think it was an invitation to walk in. If anyone but an old hen like Mrs Wilson had asked you to call on her . . .'

Quinn leaned inside the open doorway and listened. Then he said, 'She's expecting you to be alone, isn't she? Maybe it's as well you're not.'

'What are you talking about?'

'I'm not sure myself. Just strikes me it's damn funny. No one at home . . . door open . . . sitting-room lights on. After what's been going on at Denholme Court since last Saturday afternoon, I could imagine anything.'

'You're talking rubbish,' Piper said.

'Maybe. But let me ask you a question. What would you have done in these circumstances if you'd been on your own?'

It was a fair question. Piper felt a tinge of uneasiness as he listened to the empty silence of flat 1A.

In the adjoining flat the TV talked and laughed and applauded. Outside the entrance doors the rain showed no sign of slackening. Only in flat 1A was there nothing to be heard.

He said, 'I don't know what I'd have done. I didn't expect this situation to arise.'

'Could be you'd have taken a walk inside to see if something had happened to the old girl . . . eh?'

'Possibly. But if you're suggesting—'

'I'm only suggesting that it's all very fishy,' Quinn said. 'However if you want to follow your normal inclination, I'll come, too. But I won't be very close behind you . . . just in case.'

Piper said, 'You're being ridiculous—as usual. Mrs Wilson must've gone visiting one of her neighbours. That's the likeliest explanation.'

'When she's expecting you to call? And why should she leave the door unlocked. On top of all that, I got the impression when we were here the other night that she didn't do much visiting. She made quite a thing about being all alone and grasping at any bit of company she could get.'

It was true. There had been a world of loneliness in her eyes when she said, *'If you hadn't called on me, at least it would've been someone to talk to.'*

'All right,' Piper said. 'It'll be embarrassing if she comes back and finds us wandering around her flat . . . but she may have been taken ill. We'd better go and see. After all, she is an old woman.'

He pushed the door wide open and they went inside. Quinn said, 'I've got a scary feeling we might be walking into one of those things that go bump in the night. And I've just had a thought.'

'Well?'

'It's about Julian Davey. Did you tell him you'd told me how he could have killed his wife?'

'No. What's that got to do with it?'

'Maybe quite a lot. So far as he's aware you're the only one who's tumbled to his little secret.'

Piper swung round and asked, 'Are you saying he got Mrs Wilson to lay a trap for me? I've heard some crazy things—'

'OK. I won't say it. Just you be prepared for anything, that's all.'

As they approached the sitting-room, Quinn added, 'She isn't in there. I could see through the curtains. If you want my opinion she went off some place after she phoned you.'

'Right now I don't want anybody's opinion,' Piper said. 'You can have your say later.'

He went on past the sitting-room door. After another few steps, he called out, 'Mrs Wilson . . . are you there, Mrs Wilson?'

There was no sound anywhere in the flat. Quinn was right. For reasons best known to herself, Mrs Wilson had gone. Quinn was right . . . but only so far as the old lady was concerned. That other idea about Julian Davey laying a trap was sheer nonsense.

With Quinn not far behind him, Piper opened the kitchen door and reached in to switch on the light. It was a fluorescent tube and it flickered to and fro along its length before it came on.

The kitchen was clean and tidy. Mrs Wilson had obviously washed up after her evening meal and put the dishes away.

On the table lay an unwrapped joint of beef. She had not removed the paper in which it had been delivered. Piper told himself that, wherever she had gone, she must have left suddenly. The thought depressed him. Denholme Court was a twilight world he wanted to get away from.

Yet, even now, she might come back. She was bound to come back. An old woman could not just disappear . . .

He went from room to room, switching on every light and then backing out into the hall. Bedrooms . . . bathroom . . . even the toilet . . . There was no sign of Mrs Wilson anywhere in the flat.

She had unwrapped the joint of beef and left it on the table instead of putting it in the fridge. Then she had switched off the kitchen light but not the light in the sitting-room. Last of all she had so carelessly shut the outer door that it had not locked.

The whole thing was most peculiar. Mrs Wilson was not the type. At her age, women became creatures of habit. They made almost a ritual of ensuring that the outside door was properly shut.

If she were visiting a neighbour and meant to return in a minute or two she might not have troubled to put the joint in her fridge . . . and the light in the sitting-room could be intended to make a chance prowler think somebody was at home. But nothing could explain the unlocked door.

So she had not gone of her own accord . . . or fear had made her leave in sudden haste. Why she should have left and who else was involved were questions that Piper felt would best be handled by the police. If they thought he was making a mountain out of a molehill they could take whatever action they wished.

Quinn asked, 'Well? What now?'

'I'm going to phone Superintendent Rillett,' Piper said. 'The rest is up to him. If she is visiting one of her neighbours it'll be just too bad. We'll have made fools of ourselves, that's all.'

'She wouldn't go anywhere when she was expecting you.'

'It does seem unlikely. We can't go off and ignore the fact that she isn't here although she should be.'

'After what's been happening at Denholme Court you must ring the police,' Quinn said.

He waited in the hall while Piper went into the sitting-room. The outside door was still open and Quinn could hear voices and bursts of laughter from the TV in the adjoining flat. He wondered if it had to be turned up so loud because the people who lived there were hard of hearing . . . and what the other neighbours thought about it.

. . . *They'll have something else to think about if old Mrs Wilson has gone and disappeared. Damn' funny busi-*

ness. Going a bit far to imagine she's been kidnapped because she knows who killed Pauline Davey. Don't see how she could know, anyway, or she'd have mentioned it before. All she's probably got is an idea that might not be worth two hoots . . .

Then he heard Piper saying, 'Quinn, come here. I want you.'

As he went into the sitting-room he was mentally drafting a paragraph for the later editions. In the ordinary way, the disappearance of an old woman would rate no more than a few lines. But this old woman was a neighbour of two young women who had died violent deaths in the past five days.

That made her disappearance quite a story. If, of course, she had actually disappeared . . .

Then he was inside the sitting-room. And that moment brought a shock which drove all the breath out of his body. He saw why Piper had called him.

She was lying on the settee like a shapeless sack of bones, her lower jaw hanging loose, her eyelids sunken in the death-mask of her yellow raddled face. One arm trailed over the edge of the settee in mute surrender. The other hand seemed to be reaching out as though she had been trying to pull herself upright when death overtook her.

Whatever may have happened in the final seconds of her life she looked like an old, old woman who had died peacefully. Her eyes were closed, her head rested on a faded cushion. She had the air of someone who had at last yielded to the weight of her years.

Piper stood looking down at her in silence. Through the outside door came the noisy laughter of the television show.

When Quinn recovered his breath, he said, 'I never knew . . . I never had the slightest idea. From the window you can't see over the back of this thing. She was there all the time but I couldn't see her . . .'

'It wouldn't have made any difference,' Piper said. 'She must've died not long after she spoke to me on the phone.'

'Yes, I suppose so. Don't seem to be any signs of injury.

Looks as if she had a heart-attack.'

'At her age it's only to be expected. Probably didn't feel too well when she went to bring in the joint. By the time she'd unwrapped it she just managed to get in here and collapse on the settee.'

'Could explain why she wasn't so careful about shutting the door,' Quinn said.

He went into the kitchen and came back with a small hand-towel and used it to cover her face. Then he added as though talking to himself, 'Poor old biddy . . . Doesn't seem right that somebody should die all alone.'

Piper walked over to the phone. When he had dialled 999, he said, 'It's the fate of the aged in our modern society.'

Two men in a patrol car arrived within five or six minutes. Not long afterwards they were joined by a police surgeon. He asked Quinn and Piper to wait in the kitchen while he carried out his examination.

A quarter of an hour later, Dr Graham called them back into the sitting-room. Mrs Wilson's body was still on the settee but now she had been covered with a sheet that hung down to the floor.

He said, 'There are some questions I'd like to ask that may help me arrive at the cause of death. You gentlemen probably want to get off home so I won't detain you any longer than is necessary . . . but your answers could be very important. You understand, I'm sure.'

Piper said, 'Speaking for myself, I don't. But that doesn't matter. Mr Quinn and I were together all the time and we'll help in any way we can.'

'Good.' Graham took off his glasses and polished them with a crisp white handkerchief. 'Since both of you were here, you won't mind if I direct most of my questions to you, I hope?'

'Not at all. What is it you want to know?'

'Well, to start with, you can tell me if you touched the deceased or moved her or disturbed the position of the body, however slightly.'

'No, I didn't go near her. And all Quinn did was to place that little towel over her face.'

'When you entered this room she was in the same position as that in which I found her?'

'Precisely the same position.'

Dr Graham looked at Quinn and asked, 'When you went close to the settee did you see any sign that might have led you to suspect she was still alive?'

Quinn ran a hand through his tousled hair. He said, 'At the risk of being rude, that's about the daftest question I've heard in a long time. If I'd thought she was alive I wouldn't have covered her face. I'd have done something about it.'

Without any rancour, Graham asked, 'Such as what?'

'I'd have advised Mr Piper to send for an ambulance instead of reporting that an old woman had died.'

'So you were quite sure she was dead?'

'I've seen dead people before and she looked the same as all the others,' Quinn said. 'Was she dead when you got here?'

'Oh, yes. And I don't want you to get the wrong impression, Mr Quinn. I'm merely trying to clarify the situation. Did you lay the towel very lightly on her face?'

'Well, I certainly didn't clap it on like a poultice. If you'll tell me what you're driving at . . .'

Graham gave his spectacles an extra rub and put them on. When he had adjusted them very precisely, he said, 'Soon, Mr Quinn, very soon. For the moment, please bear with me.'

He turned to Piper and asked, 'What time was it when Mrs Wilson phoned you?'

'About six o'clock.'

'And you got here when?'

'Nearly seven.'

'That brackets the time of death, anyway. I arrived at seven-twenty and, in my opinion, she'd been dead something more than an hour. How did she sound on the phone?'

'The same as she'd sounded when I spoke to her in this

room last Monday night.'

'No breathlessness or any other hint of distress?'

'None that I could detect,' Piper said. 'Of course, it isn't easy to tell on the phone unless you know the person very well.'

'True.' Graham scratched the side of his neck thoughtfully. 'I just wondered. We won't be sure without a thorough PM.'

Quinn coughed. After he had patted himself on the chest, he asked, 'Sure of what?'

'If she had any form of heart disease . . . other than the degeneration one would expect in a woman of her age.'

Once again Piper had the feeling that had oppressed him while he was searching the flat. He said, 'If it wasn't her heart, what did she die from?'

'Well, now—' Dr Graham stared down at the settee with a gloomy look on his face—'that's why I'm getting in touch with Detective-Superintendent Rillett. I have little doubt that the old lady was suffocated . . . probably with the cushion I found under her head.'

CHAPTER XV

It rained on and off all Thursday night and the weather had only just begun to clear when Piper left home on Friday morning. Big Ben was striking ten o'clock as he was shown into Superintendent Rillett's office.

Quinn had already arrived. He looked better groomed than usual and more subdued. Apart from a brief greeting he seemed in no mood for talk.

The superintendent made notes of Piper's conversation with Julian Davey the previous afternoon and also his phone call from Mrs Wilson. Then Rillett said he wanted to go over once again what had happened in flat 1A from the time Piper and Quinn got there.

'... I know you've already made a fairly detailed statement but now you've slept on it you can look at the affair in retrospect. Any ideas?'

'Only one,' Quinn said. 'And you're bound to have thought of it yourself. Somebody put a cushion over the old lady's face because she was too free with her opinions. She must've advertised the fact that she could guess why Pauline Davey had been murdered ... and probably who, as well.'

Rillett thought that seemed fairly obvious. Piper said, 'I doubt if she'd have been able to put a name to the person but she must've been too close for comfort.'

'Wouldn't appear to be any other motive. So far as we're aware nothing was stolen.'

In a tone of regret, Rillett added, 'Wicked thing to smother the life out of a helpless old woman.'

Quinn asked, 'No possibility that she died from natural causes?'

'None at all. They did a PM last night and confirmed Dr Graham's findings. I've got the report here ...'

It consisted of a page and a half of foolscap. Rillett selected only as much as he thought necessary, mumbling under his breath at the parts he omitted.

'... An examination was carried out shortly before eleven o'clock. By that time, white pressure marks over the nostrils and mouth had become quite noticeable.

'To support the diagnosis of asphyxia there were also abundant petechial haemorrhages in the skin of the dead woman's face. Similar Tardieu spots were found in various internal organs . . . some capillary blood in the tissue spaces . . . oedematous fluid obstructing the bronchial tree.

'In a person of advanced years, little force is required to bring about death by suffocation . . . may have died even though the cushion believed to have been used was removed before she succumbed. Thus the possibility exists that her assailant may not have intended to cause her death but merely to prevent the deceased from crying out.

'General physical condition . . . cardiovascular system was good relative to her age . . . degenerative changes in the heart were no more than one would expect to find . . . no organic disease . . .'

Superintendent Rillett closed the folder and placed it on his desk. In a gentle voice, he said, 'Sad, isn't it? She was a pretty fit old girl and might've lived another ten years.'

'If she hadn't talked to the wrong person,' Quinn said. 'I don't think the idea was just to stop her kicking up a row. Someone couldn't afford to let her live.'

'Yes . . . but why? What could she possibly have known that we don't know?'

'Something she must've found out since Quinn and I spoke to her on Monday night,' Piper said.

He thought of the phone call just before six o'clock. She had sounded so brusque and confident.

'. . . *I think everybody's looking at it the wrong way* . . . *It was two of them. That's what I mean* . . .'

If he had not waited until Quinn rang him, it would have saved half an hour. He could have set out from Vigo Street at six instead of six-thirty. That might well have been the difference between life and death for Mrs Wilson.

But it would do no good to say anything to Quinn. The fault, if any, was not his. And it might have come to the same thing in the end. No one could be positive about the time she had died.

That was the only consolation. Whatever anybody had done it would probably have been too late.

Rillett was saying, '. . . If theft wasn't the motive, you must be right. But what did she know of such importance that she had to be shut up before she could talk?'

'I'd make a guess it was something to do with the people who live at Denholme Court,' Piper said.

'You mean Davey and Heskett?'

'Or somebody connected with them—somebody she could've identified. What I can't understand is why she talked to the one person who should never have been allowed to know what she suspected. The old woman wasn't a fool. Why would she do it?'

'I've no idea,' Rillett said. 'What I'd like someone to tell me is where Julian Davey was last night between six o'clock and six-thirty. And that doesn't mean any more than it says. I just want to have a talk with him.'

'Then you'll have to wait until he comes back,' Piper said.

'Didn't he drop any hint as to where he might be going?'

'No. He just said he'd stop anywhere he fancied. His whole idea was to get away from the events of last week-end.'

'You don't know when he was leaving London?'

'I can only assume he set off immediately after he bounced out of my office.'

'That's not to say he went very far,' Rillett said.

'He may not have gone at all. Have you inquired at his place of business?'

'Last night and again this morning. All they could tell me was that he's gone off for a few days.'

'And Heskett?'

'Oh, I've spoken to him. He says he was on his way home from the office at six o'clock. Didn't get to Denholme Court until after half-past six.'

'Of course, you've no way of proving whether that's true

or not,' Piper said.

Quinn told himself that applied equally well whichever way they turned. When Davey returned he would have an alibi. He always had an alibi. The odds were that Neil Heskett would be in the clear as well. Everybody had an alibi when the crunch came.

Except . . . The story of what had happened on Saturday afternoon ran through Quinn's mind while Piper and Superintendent Rillett went on talking.

They must already have thought what he was thinking. Davey had provided proof that he had visited the coffee shop . . . which meant he could not have left Susan Ward at Queen's Park much later than four-thirty.

. . . *Nobody's asked his former girl-friend what she did after he left her. Because she parked her car at the Armada Casino, we've all assumed she stayed put in her flat at Queen's Park from then until she went to pick up the car late Saturday evening. But that needn't be so. She might . . . she just might . . .*

That could be the answer they were all seeking. It accounted for everything—except how Susan Ward knew that Mrs Wilson had guessed the truth.

Quinn asked, 'Could a woman have suffocated the old lady?'

A shadow clouded the gentle look in Rillett's eyes. He said, 'I don't imagine you mean just any woman. Which one have you got in mind?'

'Miss Susan Ward—Davey's ex.'

'I see. Well, if she did have a hand in Mrs Wilson's death there would be only one motive. So you're suggesting that Miss Ward also murdered Pauline Davey.'

'It has to be both or neither,' Quinn said.

'That's debatable . . . but we'll leave it for the moment. The real question is why she should kill Davey's wife.'

'To get her out of the way so that Susan and Julian could wipe out the mistakes of the past and live happily ever after.'

With the faintest hint of a smile on his big solemn face,

Rillett said, 'You surprise me. I'd never thought you, of all people, had old-fashioned ideas. That type of motive for murder went out of vogue a long time ago.'

'Only so far as conspiracy between husband and mistress is concerned. I know that nowadays convention doesn't stop a man going off with another woman. But disposal of the wife by the mistress is still quite popular in cases where the husband either doesn't believe in divorce or dislikes publicity or has a thing about living in sin . . . to coin a phrase.'

Superintendent Rillett said, 'The subtle distinction between having a mistress and living in sin escapes me. However . . .'

'She might not be his mistress—yet,' Quinn said. 'But my impression is that she'd jump at the chance of marrying him. I've given you several reasons why Pauline Davey could have been an obstacle to that end. It's just a suggestion, of course, nothing more.'

'Of course . . .'

Almost apologetically, Rillett went on, 'I don't want to steal your thunder but I have had similar thoughts about Miss Ward myself. They never got me very far because I kept coming up against the lack of a solid motive. Apart from that, she doesn't seem the type to stab another woman to death.'

'Is there any special type?'

'Perhaps not. It isn't really important, anyway. The main thing is motive. We haven't got one strong enough to stand up on its own.'

He looked at Piper and asked, 'What do you think?'

Piper said, 'I'm inclined to agree. If Davey were a poor man and his wife had been insured or possessed money in her own right, it would be different. But he seems to be in a prosperous way of business.'

'We checked that angle—and he is. The question of getting his freedom hardly arises, either. Even if his wife refused to divorce him he had only to wait a relatively short time and divorce would be automatic.'

'Unless it's against his principles,' Quinn said. 'I don't want to flog a dead horse but we can't ignore the possibility that Susan Ward knew his feelings on the matter and took the only course open to her.'

'That would mean she had a key to the flat. Where did she get it? From Davey? It's a strange man who's opposed to divorce on principle and yet enters into a conspiracy to murder.'

The recollection of Davey passing the sitting-room door was in Piper's mind again as he added, 'If we discount the fact that she couldn't have got in without a key, we still have to explain something else—the weapon that was used. Unless Davey told her, how would she know about the pair of scissors on the bedside table?'

Superintendent Rillett said, 'The answer is that she couldn't have known. Only one person was in a position to know—Julian Davey.'

'No, he wasn't the only one,' Piper said. 'You're forgetting Heskett. Saturday afternoon wasn't the first time he'd been in Mrs Davey's bedroom.'

With a cynical grin, Quinn said, 'Now we're back to square one. Davey or Heskett . . . Heskett or Davey . . . Tweedledum and Tweedledee. You choose your fancy and you takes your pick. All we know for a fact is that Pauline Davey was murdered. All we're saying is that nobody had a motive for killing her. In a case like this, Superintendent, I wish you the best of luck.'

'I'll need that and more,' Rillett said. 'The trouble really is that several people had a motive—a very inadequate motive with the exception of her husband if he'd learned she was in the habit of sleeping with a friendly neighbour.'

Piper said, 'Unfortunately, he couldn't have done it because he was elsewhere at the time she was killed.'

'So he had no reason to be afraid of anything Mrs Wilson might've found out.'

'But somebody had a very good reason. The old lady wasn't suffocated for fun.'

Quinn said, 'Now who's being old-fashioned? Why don't

you get groovy, man, and use the in talk? You mean for the kicks.'

'I mean—' Rillett sighed—'we're not dealing with a homicidal maniac who kills for the sake of killing. Mrs Wilson's phone call last night to Mr Piper rules that out. Accidentally or otherwise, she must've discovered something we're still looking for. If her week-end joint hadn't arrived at that very moment . . .'

'She'd be alive today,' Piper said.

'Pity she wasn't a vegetarian.' Quinn began feeling in his raincoat pockets. 'On the other hand, I think she'd have made some excuse to get you to visit her. She fancied you . . . in a motherly fashion, of course. She even said you reminded her of her late husband. You were an understanding man like he had been and she wished you could stay for a while but she supposed . . .'

A faraway look came into Quinn's eyes. With both hands in his pockets he sat staring into the middle-distance as though listening to something that he alone could hear.

Then he turned slowly to Rillett and asked, 'Did you say nothing had been stolen?'

'So far as we're aware. According to her son she didn't have much of value in the flat.'

'And on the phone—' Quinn looked at Piper—'she told you she thought everybody was looking at it the wrong way. Is that right?'

'Yes . . . but we've been all through it before—'

'From the wrong angle,' Quinn said. 'I've got a feeling I know what she meant when she said it was two of them.'

He stood up abruptly. As he walked to the door, he added, 'You'll excuse me, won't you?'

Superintendent Rillett asked, 'Where are you going?'

'To see a pretty lady,' Quinn said.

CHAPTER XVI

PIPER SPENT the rest of the morning clearing up arrears of work. He had plenty to do and it was useless to fritter away his time speculating on where Quinn had gone or the identity of the woman he had talked about. He would explain when he felt inclined to do so . . . and not before.

Lunchtime came and went. Piper got back to the office at two o'clock and began dealing with the day's correspondence. If there were no distractions he hoped to be completely up-to-date by evening. Then he would have the weekend free.

Nothing to do for two whole days. Maybe he would take Jane shopping, have dinner in town and see a show. Not like last Saturday . . . He pushed that disturbing thought out of his mind.

It was half-past two when Quinn phoned. He said, 'Ah, glad I've caught you in. I was afraid you might still be wallowing in your usual five-course lunch.'

Piper asked, 'Where have you been?'

'I told you before I left the Super's office. I had a sudden yearning for the company of a certain pretty lady.'

'Don't tax my patience too much. Who is this woman and what has she got to do with the affair at Denholme Court?'

'No need to bully me,' Quinn said. 'Answer one: her name is Janet Wrexham and she lives in flat 3B. Answer two: a lot. Any other questions?'

'Yes . . . but I've neither the time nor the inclination for your kind of nonsense.'

'That's what the curate said on his wedding night . . . OK, OK, don't hang up. You'll be sorry if you do. I know the meaning of Mrs Wilson's cryptic remark to you on the phone.'

'About there being two of them?'

'Yes. What's more, I've gone a stage further than she got. I'm fairly sure I can name the second one. With a little help from you the rest shouldn't be too difficult . . . as the old duke said to the nursemaid. And I'm not telling you another thing until we meet.'

'Then we won't meet,' Piper said. 'This is one of my busy afternoons and I don't feel disposed to squander it on the strength of nothing but talk. Either you give me some idea what this is all about or you'll get no help from me.'

Quinn said, 'Them's fightin' words. But I suppose you're right. The thing is that I'm feeling kind of pleased with myself and this is my way of blowing off steam. Can't I persuade you to take me on trust?'

'Not entirely. I want something tangible before I throw away an afternoon's work.'

'It won't be thrown away. Have I ever let you down?'

Arguing with Quinn was like shooting into a suspended blanket. Piper said, 'This isn't going to be the first time. Why did you call on Mrs Wrexham?'

'To ask her a couple of questions.'

'And?'

'She gave me the answers I'd anticipated.'

'Which were . . . ?'

'One was yes. The other has still to be proved . . . although I haven't the slightest doubt she's telling the truth. With a bit of luck, Sherwood, the caretaker, will confirm what Mrs Wrexham says. Then, with your co-operation, we'll be on the home straight.'

'And all this has come about because nothing was stolen from the old woman's flat?'

'Indirectly—yes.'

Piper said, 'I won't pretend that I understand what you're saying. I seldom do and—'

'Thanks.'

'—and I should insist on getting real answers—not conundrums. You realize that, don't you?'

'Only if you're so mentally lazy you want it served up on a plate,' Quinn said. 'I had to think it out for myself. With the greatest respect, Mr Piper, sir, why shouldn't you?'

The time had come to give in. Piper asked, 'Where are you speaking from?'

'A phone box not far from Cornstalk Avenue. After I'd called on Mrs Wrexham at her shop in the Finchley Road I took a walk here and there and chatted with various people—including the landlord of a very nice pub. I haven't had a better pint in months.'

'You should eat more and drink less.'

'Yes, sir . . . whatever you say, sir. As it happens I had a sandwich. Acts as an alcoholic blotter. When I left the hostelry I was feeling pretty good until I nearly got knocked down by some fool in a sports car. Came blinding into the car-park like the Mad Mullah. It took another pint to settle my palpitations.'

'Any excuse is better than none,' Piper said. 'Where do you want me to meet you?'

Quinn had a bout of coughing. His voice was still wheezy when he said, 'Did you hear about the lady driver who swerved to avoid a child and fell out of bed? No? Then I'll tell you about it some time when I'm not so busy.'

'Where do you want me to meet you?'

'Oh, yes, of course. That would be useful. I'll be inside or in the neighbourhood of the phone box.'

'All right . . . but I hope you're not getting me out to Hampstead on a fool's errand.'

In a changed voice, Quinn said, 'I can't give any guarantee. But I'll tell you this for nothing. I'm not crying over Pauline Davey. What cuts me up is that poor old lass fighting for her life with not a soul to help her.'

He coughed again. Then he added, 'I'll leave you with this thought. The moral to my tale is that when you gamble you're bound to lose . . . one way or another. 'Bye for now.'

It had begun to rain by the time Piper reached Belsize Lane. As he got nearer Cornstalk Avenue he saw that someone was using the coinbox phone—a youth with metal-rimmed spectacles, a big head of fuzzy hair and a beard that left little more than his nose and eyes exposed. He held the phone in one hand and a sandwich in the other. Quinn was sheltering in the lee of the box, his raincoat collar up to his ears. When he caught sight of Piper he trotted across the pavement, his hands in his pockets, rain dripping off his lank hair.

He had trouble opening the car door. When he got in he shook himself like a dog and mopped his face and neck with a damp handkerchief. He looked chilled and miserable.

As the car pulled away, he said, 'Did you see that gollywog in the phone box? Damn' glad he had something to eat or he might've roasted me over the tribal campfire. If I were an anthropologist I'd say he was a throw-back to the primitive aborigines but he hadn't been thrown back far enough . . . Took you a long time to get here, didn't it?'

Piper said, 'Just over twenty minutes isn't bad. Not my fault it's raining. You should've chosen a better meeting place.'

'Who says it's your fault? Who's complaining? Can't I ask a simple question without getting my head bitten off?'

He gave his face another wipe and stuffed the handkerchief in an outside pocket. Then he grinned, looked at Piper wide-eyed and asked, 'What'll you do if this turns out to be a wild-goose chase?'

'Nothing. With someone like you there's always that risk. I won't shoot you. Won't be the first time you've had a bee in your bonnet.'

'Very handsome of you,' Quinn said. 'This time I think you'll find somebody else is going to get stung.'

With rain streaming off the windscreen wipers they drove along Cornstalk Avenue until they saw the twin blocks of Denholme Court under a sullen sky: white window frames, trim lawns bordered by colourful autumn flowers. There was a delivery van parked outside the second entrance.

As he edged into the kerb Piper was thinking of the night he had come here to talk to Julian Davey and found him in Heskett's flat. It would have served no purpose to ask how long the affair with Pauline had been going on.

That moment of truth was sharp and clear in Piper's mind—the moment when Heskett's real emotions showed through all his deception and bluff. What he had said could have been his confession of faith.

'... She was a wonderful person ... I'd never met anyone like her. What made me behave as I did is something I won't even try to explain. You can despise me all you want ... I'm not sorry for what I did.'

Strange how Davey's grief had been blunted by the knowledge that his wife had betrayed him. Yet ... perhaps not so strange. Perhaps their marriage would have ended sooner or later even without the intervention of Neil Heskett. Ended ... or dragged on as a mere pretence when the spirit was dead.

She had made a habit of going out alone. Those visits to the Armada Casino could have been an illustration that their lives were drifting apart. Heskett was her temporary means of escape from a husband who was, in one way or anothe, inadequate.

The time might have come when Davey would have sought his freedom. Now he was free. Piper wondered how long it would be before Susan Ward went seeking his company.

... Soon enough the tangle of relationships will be unravelled. Those who were closest to her will forget Pauline Davey ... and Heskett's wife who died unloved ... and a lonely old woman who had earned the right to end her days in peace ...

Pauline had dragged them all down with her—Pauline who was a grey shadow hovering behind the lives of those enmeshed in her death. As a person she would soon be forgotten. As a shadow there would be no rest until the secret of her last afternoon was solved.

She had been about to die when Davey was talking over old times with a woman called Susan Ward. If Davey had gone straight home ...

Once again, Susan was saying '... *Whether you believe me or not, I can assure you I'll never see him again.*'

So much lying, so much cheating, and then the culmination when death opened the door of flat 2A. Heskett had used a key that Pauline had given his wife—the key that was kept on a hook in the kitchen of his own flat. At the inquest, Davey had said there were only two keys. He still had his own and his wife's key had been in her handbag when he went to look for it.

Pauline had never told him about the spare key. Providing Deborah Heskett with one was a clever stratagem. Any time she was out, her husband could take the key off its hook and slip into flat 2A.

Davey had not known about that third key. Even if he had it would have made no difference. The two wives had exchanged keys in case either of them was out when a tradesman called. Nothing in that to arouse Julian's suspicion.

So there had been three keys—not two. It was another example of the deception which tainted everyone who had come in contact with Pauline Davey. Three keys ...

As the car came to a halt Piper seemed to hear the echo of his own voice when he and Rillett and Quinn talked together in the superintendent's office. It had no association with those three keys and yet he knew it must, in some way, be connected.

'... *If Davey were a poor man and his wife had been insured or possessed money in her own right* ...'

Like the upheaval of a silent explosion all Piper's false ideas disintegrated. He knew why Quinn had asked if Rillett were sure nothing had been stolen from old Mrs Wilson's flat, he knew the one question that Quinn must have asked Mrs Wrexham, the attractive widow in flat 3B.

Quinn was saying '... You've gone into one of your trances again. If I were you I'd see a doctor. Could be awkward if it happened when you were driving in heavy traffic. I've spoken to you twice but you weren't at home.'

'I'm sorry,' Piper said. 'My mind was elsewhere.'

'Oh, I know that without you telling me. I was only worried in case it didn't come back. Sure you're all right?'

'Don't be silly. If Sherwood confirms the second thing Mrs Wrexham told you what are you going to do next?'

'Do?' Quinn twiddled his fingers and looked coy. 'Well, now, I think I'll just play it by ear.'

They got out of the car and hurried into the right-hand block of flats. Quinn led the way to the far door opening on to the gardens at the rear.

Piper asked, 'Where's the caretaker likely to be?'

'Couldn't say. The first time I called at Denholme Court he was out here. We'll have to scout around and hope for the best.'

Rain danced on the surface of the swimming pool, rain glistened on the evergreen bushes. The tiled paths were shining wet.

Quinn said, 'He may be over at the garages. You can shelter under the trees, if you like, while I take a look.'

It was reasonably dry underfoot when they reached the clump of trees. Where the branches interlaced the rain had not yet penetrated. And they had no need to go any further. The door of the garden shed was open.

Through the dusty window facing the path they could see Sherwood. He was seated on a box with a mug of tea in one hand and a folded newspaper in the other.

As they trudged through the layer of fallen leaves he looked up. For a moment he sat watching them. Then he put down his mug and came to the door.

With a pleasant look on his weatherbeaten face he nodded to Piper and wished him a good afternoon. He ignored Quinn.

'. . . What can I do for you, sir?'

Piper said, 'If we may come inside . . .'

'Yes, of course, sir. Not much room, I'm afraid, but at least you'll be out of the wet.'

They squeezed into the shed after Sherwood made more space by putting the box in a corner on top of the sacks of fertilizer. Then he said, 'I hope you're not going to talk about Mrs Wilson. She was a nice old lady and it gave me quite a turn when she died sudden like. You'd almost imagine somebody'd put a jinx on this place.'

'Three deaths in less than a week must be a bit upsetting,' Piper said.

'You can say that again, sir. Mrs Wilson spoke to me lunchtime yesterday and I'd have sworn there wasn't a thing wrong with her.'

'There wasn't,' Quinn said.

Sherwood stared at him and asked, 'What's that supposed to mean?'

'She was all right at lunchtime yesterday. For your information she was all right at six o'clock yesterday. But I can appreciate how you feel and so we won't pursue it. Instead I'd like you to answer a question about—'

'No, just you hold on.' Sherwood's eyes flitted to Piper and back to Quinn again. 'We will pursue it. You can keep your question until I know what's going on. Why do you say she was all right at six o'clock? When I got here this morning one of the tenants told me Mrs Wilson must've died some time just after six.'

'But not because there had been anything wrong with her health,' Quinn said. 'You'll hear about it pretty soon and so I may as well tell you. The old lady would be alive now if she hadn't been suffocated.'

The caretaker wiped a hand across his face, looked at Piper and asked, 'Is that true, sir?'

Piper said, 'I'm sorry to say it is.'

'How—' Sherwood shook his head—'how did it happen?'

'Somebody held a cushion over her face,' Quinn said.

Swift disbelief puckered the caretaker's eyes. He said, 'No, that can't be. Nobody'd do a thing like that to old Mrs Wilson. She was as good as gold. Everyone liked her. Must be some mistake.'

'Not a chance. The results of a post mortem last night confirmed it. If you'd like to help the police catch the party who killed her . . .'

'I'm damn sure I would. But I don't see how I can. The

last time I saw Mrs Wilson was at lunch time . . . like I say.'

'This isn't about Mrs Wilson,' Quinn said. 'It concerns the tenant in 3B.'

'Mrs Wrexham?'

'Yes. You've heard, I suppose, that Heskett and Mrs Davey were carrying on together?'

Sherwood nodded. He said, 'There's been enough talk about it. I didn't know how near the mark I was when I saw him outside her door that morning. You remember I mentioned the way she looked at him?'

'Sure. That's what first put the idea in my head. Then Mrs Wrexham clinched it . . .'

Piper listened with only part of his mind. He should have thought of it himself the night Quinn repeated what the young widow had said. For that matter, so should Superintendent Rillett when Sergeant Langdon reported his conversation with Mrs Wrexham.

The old lady had been right. She had seen further than everybody else. All of them had looked at it the wrong way.

'. . . *It was two of them. That's what I mean . . .*'

So near the truth . . . but not near enough. The tragedy was that she had not phoned just five minutes earlier.

Sherwood was asking '. . . Do you mean Mrs Wrexham knew what was going on between them two?'

'No, not that,' Quinn said. 'Something much more important. She says you can confirm that she told Heskett what happened at the Armada Casino last Friday night.'

'At the casino? I don't get that. What did happen?'

'Mrs Davey won quite a lot of money. Seems Mrs Wrexham was there and heard about it. On Saturday morning she met Heskett when she went to the garage to get her car . . . and she said something to him about Mrs Davey's winning streak.'

With a puzzled look, Sherwood asked, 'Where's all this getting us?'

'Depends on whether Mrs Wrexham's mistaken or not. I can't see why she should tell lies . . . but she could be confusing Heskett with somebody else. And that's where you can settle this thing one way or the other. She says you were around at the time and you may have heard what she was saying to him.'

'Supposing I did?'

'Then Mister Neil Heskett won't have a cat-in-hell chance of denying it,' Quinn said.

The puzzled look in Sherwood's eyes changed to scepticism. He said, 'As it happens, I did hear her mention it. I was cleaning her windscreen when Heskett came across to her and she didn't lower her voice or anything. The way she spoke it was no secret. And in my opinion—'

'Skip that for the moment. Would you be willing to stand up in court and swear you were present when Mrs Wrexham told Neil Heskett about Mrs Davey's big win the night before?'

It took the caretaker only a few seconds to make up his mind. In an abrupt tone, he said, 'If I had to—yes. All the same, I think you're barking up the wrong tree. Mr Heskett isn't short of money. He wouldn't kill Mrs Davey for the sake of four hundred pounds.'

'No . . . but you would,' Quinn said.

For what seemed an endless time, Sherwood stood rigid and still, his mouth open, his eyes seeking a place to hide. All the blood had drained out of his face.

Then in little stiff movements he turned his head and looked at Piper. No one spoke. There was only the sound of the rain on the trees.

Sherwood at last found his voice. With his eyes clinging to Piper's face, he asked, 'What—what's he talking about?'

'You don't need me to tell you,' Piper said. 'All three of us know what happened last Saturday afternoon. You murdered Pauline Davey because she woke up and found you searching for the money she'd won at the casino.'

'It's—' the caretaker moistened his lips—'it's a lie. You're covering up for somebody else . . . that's what you're both doing. I'll see a lawyer and stop you saying things like that.'

Piper said, 'No lawyer can save you now. We had all

the pieces right from the beginning and it shouldn't have taken us so long to put them together. We eliminated theft as a motive because there was a large sum of money in the bedroom and it hadn't been stolen. No one thought that the thief might've been interrupted and could only get away by killing Mrs Davey.'

'I didn't do it.' Sherwood was breathing fast and he had difficulty in controlling his voice. 'I can prove I didn't do it. I was in Mrs Wilson's flat all afternoon until at least half-past five.'

'Except for a few minutes around five o'clock. Mrs Wilson brewed a pot of tea for you about a quarter to five. She went back to her seat at the front room window no later than ten to five. You weren't seen by her between then and probably a little before five-fifteen. She told us you were in the sitting-room fixing one of the window catches at a quarter past five when Mrs Heskett returned home.'

'She also told us you'd mentioned seeing Davey drive out of the garage at half-past one,' Quinn said. 'The mistake you made was in thinking he'd driven round to the front entrance and picked up his wife. You thought there'd be no one in the flat until evening.'

In a sudden burst of violence, Sherwood said, 'It's a trick! The whole thing's a trick! But you won't get away with it. When I've talked to a lawyer—'

'Better see he's a good one. You're going to need the best . . . because the only trick was the stunt you pulled. If your alibi hadn't come unstuck you'd have got away with it.'

'I've done nothing to be afraid of! You can't prove I wasn't in Mrs Wilson's sitting-room at five o'clock when that Davey woman was killed. You just try and see where it gets—'

'I'll take that chance,' Quinn said. 'Because you can't prove you were in the old lady's flat. There's only your word for it. She's dead. You killed your own alibi last night when you shut her mouth with a cushion.'

A numb look settled on Sherwood's weatherbeaten face.

Step by step he went back until his shoulders bumped into some garden tools hanging on the wall. Then he groped behind him with one hand as though feeling for an exit that was not there.

Piper said, 'I can understand what happened on Saturday afternoon. You panicked. My guess is that Mrs Davey snatched up the scissors and you used them against her because you'd lost control of yourself. By the time you realized what you had done it was too late.'

'But with old Mrs Wilson it wasn't like that,' Quinn said. 'It wasn't like that at all. When she got the idea that two different people had visited the Daveys' flat for two different motives she did something very foolish: she called you in and tried out her theory on you. She didn't know . . .'

What was left of Sherwood's resistance flared momentarily in his eyes and then went out. He slumped against the wall, his arms dangling as though they were too heavy to support.

'. . . God help her, she didn't know,' Quinn went on, 'When I think of what you did to her I only wish they'd bring back the death penalty . . . just once . . . just for you.'

The old woman was talking inside Piper's head. He could hear her saying '. . . *I wouldn't let him finish the odds and ends on Sunday out of respect for my neighbours and so he came in again tonight . . . If you hadn't called on me, at least it would've been someone to talk to.*'

He should not have waited for Quinn to join him. He should have gone to Denholme Court without wasting any time. His delay had cost Mrs Wilson her life.

Regret was futile. It served no purpose to bewail a lost opportunity, to damn himself because of the might-have-been.

Sherwood had begun rocking from side to side. His eyes held nothing but despair.

Without moving his lips, he mumbled, 'Go away . . . it's a lie . . . it's all lies . . .'

He sagged lower, his head bent, his face twitching. He looked like a man deranged.

Quinn turned away from him and asked, 'Which of us is going to phone the police?'

'You can do it,' Piper said. 'I'll stay here.'

'Will you be all right?'

'Oh, yes. He won't get away. For his sake, I hope he won't try.'

Quinn said, 'You're too charitable.'

Before he reached the door there was the sound of footsteps on the tiled path leading to the clump of trees. Through the rain he saw two men who looked familiar.

As they passed the swimming pool he recognized them. Over his shoulder he grinned at Piper and said, 'The hill has come to Mahomet. We're getting visitors.'

They came trudging through the fallen leaves at a steady, unhurried pace, the superintendent three or four steps ahead of Sergeant Langdon. As they came nearer Quinn went to meet them.

He said, 'Glad to see you, Superintendent. You've restored my faith in officialdom . . . and chastened my sinful vanity. I'd begun to think I was a clever boy.'

'Humility doesn't suit you,' Rillett said.

With just the hint of a smile on his big solemn face, he added, 'Let me say you're not as big a fool as you often sound.'

Quinn said, 'I'm not stopping you. Put it in writing and I might get a rise.'

'Remind me—' Rillett's smile had gone as he stooped to go into the shed—'when I've settled this business.'

Sherwood seemed unaware of his surroundings. It was as though he could neither see nor hear. He still drooped against the wall where the tools hung from a row of hooks.

After he had given him a long, cold look, the superintendent turned to Piper and asked, 'What does he have to say for himself?'

'Denies it . . . as you'd expect.'

'Of course. But he'll soon change his tune when I've had a nice quiet chat with him all by ourselves. How long do you think he'd go on denying it if I told him he was seen coming out of Mrs Wilson's flat at twenty past six last night?'

Piper said, 'That's all you need.'

Very slowly the caretaker looked up. In a dazed tone, he said, 'It's a lie . . . it's all lies. There was nobody around when I—'

His mouth remained open and terror filled his eyes. After a moment he covered them with both hands. Then he began to wail in a wild demented voice. With tears squeezing out between his fingers he went on wailing.

CHAPTER XVII

At lunchtime on Saturday there was the usual jostling crowd in the Three Feathers. When Piper arrived just after one-fifteen he had to push his way through the noisy congestion of the lounge bar.

Quinn was perched on a stool in his favourite corner. He asked, 'What'll you have?'

'It's my turn,' Piper said. 'Seems a long time since I bought you a drink.'

'That's because it is a long time. Freddie!'

The barman limped towards them, his weasel face puckered in a scowl. He said, 'It's got so's I hear that voice in my dreams.'

'I never knew—' Quinn emptied his glass—'knew you cared. Fetch me another pint of your vintage bitter and serve my friend with anything he's willing to pay for.'

'Haven't you got any manners?'

'Yes . . . mainly bad ones. What I haven't got is any beer. So do you think we might get a bit of service?'

Freddie said, 'I know what you should get.'

He refilled Quinn's glass, brought Piper a whisky and thanked him for the tip. '. . . Always knew you were a gentleman, sir. Just goes to prove you can't judge people by the company they keep.'

'Don't tempt me,' Quinn said. 'I don't know my own strength . . . and I've been thrown out of better pubs than this one.'

Someone called Freddie to the other end of the bar. When he had gone, Piper said, 'I liked your column this morning. One of the best things you've done.'

'Thanks. Praise from you is praise indeed.'

'Well, I mean it. Seen anything of the superintendent?'

'Not since our jamboree in the garden shed. Spoke to him on the phone, of course. Taken all round he's not a

bad fellow. I've grown to like old Solemn Sammy.'
'Did he say how much progress he's made with Sherwood?'
'Not in so many words . . . but I gather it's just about all sewn up. Here's to your good health.'
Quinn took a long drink, smacked his lips and put down the glass. Then he looked towards the door and his face changed.
He said, 'Well, well, well! Talk of the angels and you hear the clump of their number tens. Look who's come slumming.'
Superintendent Rillett edged his way through the crush and joined them. He said, 'I didn't expect to see you, Mr Piper. I thought Quinn would be here on his own. A little bird told me he was usually in the Three Feathers about this time.'
'I'll bet that little bird's got big feet and calls to its mate with a police whistle,' Quinn said.
'You could be right. Anyway, I've come specially because I'd like to buy you a drink. Can't stay long. So what's it going to be?'
'You've come—' there was a look of wonderment on Quinn's thin pale face—'you've come specially to buy me a drink? What have I done to deserve this signal honour?'
Very hastily, he added, 'Not that I'm questioning your good judgment for one moment. Soon as my glass is empty I'll have the same again.'
'And you, Mr Piper?'
'This is my round,' Piper said.
'No . . . please.' Rillett beckoned to the barman. 'I'm grateful to both of you and this is the only way I can show my appreciation? Do you mind?'
'Not at all. But let's be honest. You weren't far off the real answer yourself, were you?'
The superintendent shrugged. With a smile warming the gentle look in his eyes, he said, 'Well, in my job I always believe in leaving open as many options as I can. But it will still be my pleasure to buy you a drink.'

'And mine to accept it,' Quinn said. 'But no hurry. They used to say one at a time was good fishing.'

The barman was occupied with a fresh group of customers. While he waited, Rillett said, 'You may be interested to know I've heard from Davey. He got in touch with his office this morning and they told him to phone me.'

Piper asked, 'Did he have anything useful to contribute?'

'Yes, one thing that should strengthen my case . . . if the defence enters a plea of not guilty.'

'Which is quite possible.'

'Oh, yes. Happens more often than not. However, Davey says his wife occasionally loaned her key to Sherwood. There were times when she was in town for the day and he had to pop in and out of the flat on maintenance work.'

'Easy enough to have a copy made,' Quinn said.

He took a mouthful of beer and swallowed it down with another mouthful. Then he added, 'I keep thinking about Mrs Heskett. She was the odd one out, wasn't she?'

'Yes . . . and odd is the right word. I've been talking to Heskett again and he says his wife could be very erratic. Must've been brooding for quite a while over the affair between her husband and her friend.'

'And she jumped to the wrong conclusion when Pauline came to a bad end.'

'That was all she needed to push her over the edge,' Rillett said. 'I wonder how Heskett manages to live with himself?'

Piper remembered the confrontation in flat 2C. Through his thoughts he could hear Neil Heskett saying '. . . *She was a wonderful person . . . I've never met anyone like her . . .*'

He said, 'I'm not sure if an outsider is entitled to sit in judgment. We don't know what life has been like for Neil Heskett. Not all marriages are made in heaven.'

Quinn said, 'Amen. Here endeth the first lesson . . .'

Then Freddie took their order . . . and brought a round of drinks . . . and Rillet raised his glass in salute. All around them there was noisy talk and bursts of laughter.

After a long silence Quinn looked up at the clock behind the bar. In a subdued voice, he said, 'You know what? It's one-thirty. At this time, exactly one week ago, a man called Julian Davey was leaving his flat in Denholme Court.'

Piper asked, 'What's so profound in that thought?'

'Nothing very much.' Quinn took a long drink and put his glass down carefully. 'I was just thinking that this past week would've turned out very different for a lot of people if Arsenal hadn't been playing at home last Saturday . . . wouldn't it?'